COLLECTION 12

COLLECTION 12

The Headless Ghost
The Abominable Snowman of Pasadena
How I Got My Shrunken Head

R.L. Stine

Hippo

Scholastic Children's Books,
Commonwealth House, 1–19 New Oxford Street, London WC1A 1NU, UK
A division of Scholastic Ltd
London ~ New York ~ Toronto ~ Sydney ~ Auckland
Mexico City ~ New Delhi ~ Hong Kong

First published in this edition by Scholastic Ltd, 1999

The Headless Ghost
The Abominable Snowman of Pasadena
First published in the USA by Scholastic Inc., 1995
First published in the UK by Scholastic Ltd, 1997
How I Got My Shrunken Head
First published in the USA by Scholastic Inc., 1996
First published in the UK by Scholastic Ltd, 1997

Copyright © Parachute Press Inc., 1995, 1996
GOOSEBUMPS is a trademark of Parachute Press, Inc.

ISBN 0 590 11382 8
All rights reserved

Typeset by Rowland Phototypesetting Ltd, Bury St Edmunds, Suffolk
Printed by Cox & Wyman Ltd, Reading, Berks.

10 9 8 7 6 5 4 3 2 1

CONTENTS

The Headless Ghost

Stephanie Alpert and I haunt our neighbourhood.

We got the idea last Hallowe'en.

There are a lot of kids in our neighbourhood, and we like to haunt them and give them a little scare.

Sometimes we sneak out late at night in masks and stare into kids' windows. Sometimes we leave rubber hands and rubber fingers on windowsills. Sometimes we hide disgusting things in letterboxes.

Sometimes Stephanie and I duck down behind bushes or trees and make the most frightening sounds—animal howls and ghostly moans. Stephanie can do a terrifying werewolf howl. And I can toss back my head and shriek loud enough to shake the leaves on the trees.

We keep almost all the kids on our block pretty frightened.

In the mornings, we catch them peeking out

3

of their doors, seeing if it's safe to come out. And at night, most of them are afraid to leave their houses alone.

Stephanie and I are really proud of that.

During the day we are just Stephanie Alpert and Duane Comack, two normal twelve-year-olds. But at night, we become the Twin Terrors of Wheeler Falls.

No one knows. No one.

Look at us, and you see two sixth graders at Wheeler Middle School. Both of us have brown eyes and brown hair. Both of us are tall and thin. Stephanie is a few inches taller because she has higher hair.

Some people see us hanging out together and think we're brother and sister. But we're not. We don't have any brothers and sisters, and we don't mind one bit.

We live across the street from one another. We walk to school together in the morning. We usually swap lunches, even though our parents pack both of us peanut-butter-and-jelly sandwiches.

We're normal. Totally normal.

Except for our secret late-night hobby.

How did we become the Twin Terrors? Well, it's sort of a long story. . .

Last Hallowe'en was a cool, clear night. A full moon floated over the bare trees.

I was standing outside Stephanie's front window in my scary Grim Reaper costume. I stood up on tiptoes, trying to peek inside to check out her costume.

"Hey—beat it, Duane! No looking!" she shouted through the closed window. Then she pulled down the shade.

"I wasn't looking. I was just stretching!" I shouted back.

I was eager to see what Stephanie was going to be. Every Hallowe'en she comes up with something awesome. The year before, she came waddling out inside a huge ball of green toilet paper. You guessed it. She was an iceberg lettuce.

But this year I thought maybe I had beaten her.

I'd worked really hard on my Grim Reaper costume. I wore high platform shoes—so high that I'd tower over Stephanie. My black, hooded cape swung along the ground. I hid my curly brown hair under a tight rubber skullcap. And I smeared my face with sick-looking make-up, the colour you see on mouldy bread.

My dad didn't want to look at me. He said I turned his stomach.

A success!

I couldn't wait to make Stephanie sick! I banged my Grim Reaper sickle on Stephanie's window. "Hey, Steph—hurry up!" I called. "I'm getting hungry. I want sweets!"

I waited and waited. I started pacing back and forth across her front lawn, my long cape sweeping over the grass and dead leaves.

"Hey! Where are you?" I called again.

No Stephanie.

With an impatient groan, I turned back to the house.

And a huge, hairy animal jumped me from behind and chewed off my head.

Well, it didn't *really* chew off my head.

But it tried to.

It growled and tried to sink its gleaming fangs into my throat.

I staggered back. The creature looked like an enormous black cat, covered in thick, black bristles. Gobs of yellow goo poured from its hairy ears and black nose. Its long, pointed fangs glowed in the dark.

The creature snarled again and shot out a hairy paw. "Sweets . . . give me all your sweets!"

"Stephanie—?" I choked out. It *was* Stephanie. Wasn't it?

The creature jabbed its claws into my stomach in reply. That's when I recognized Stephanie's Mickey Mouse watch on its hairy wrist.

"Wow. Stephanie, you look great! You really—" I didn't finish. Stephanie ducked behind the hedge and yanked me down beside her.

My knees hit the pavement hard. "Ow! Are you crazy?" I shrieked. "What's the big idea?"

A group of little kids in costumes paraded by. Stephanie leapt out of the hedge. "Arrrggghhh!" she growled.

The little kids totally freaked. They turned and started to run. Three of them dropped their trick-or-treat bags. Stephanie scooped up the bags. "Yummmm!"

"Whoa! You really scared them," I said, watching the little kids run up the street. "That was cool."

Stephanie started to laugh. She has a high, silly laugh that always starts me laughing, too. It sounds like a chicken being tickled. "That was really good fun," she replied. "More fun than trick-or-treating."

So we spent the rest of the night scaring kids.

We didn't get many sweets. But we had a great time.

"I wish we could do this every night!" I exclaimed as we walked home.

"We can," Stephanie said, grinning. "It doesn't have to be Hallowe'en to scare kids, Duane. Get my meaning?"

I got her meaning.

She tossed back her bristly head and let out her chicken laugh. And I laughed, too.

And that's how Stephanie and I started haunting our neighbourhood. Late at night, the Twin Terrors strike, up and down our neighbourhood. We're *everywhere*!

Well. . . *almost* everywhere.

There's one place in our neighbourhood that even Stephanie and I are afraid of.

It's an old stone house on the next block. It's called Hill House. I guess that's because it sits up on a high hill on Hill Street.

I know. I know. A lot of towns have a haunted house.

But Hill House really is haunted.

Stephanie and I know that for sure.

Because that's where we met the Headless Ghost.

Hill House is the biggest tourist attraction in Wheeler Falls. Actually, it's the *only* one.

Maybe you've heard of Hill House. It's written up in a lot of books.

Tour guides in creepy black uniforms give the Hill House tour every hour. The guides will act real scary and tell frightening stories about the house. Some of the ghost stories give me cold shivers.

Stephanie and I love to take the tour—especially with Otto. Otto is our favourite guide.

Otto is big and bald and scary-looking. He has tiny black eyes that seem to stare right through you. And he has a booming voice that comes from deep inside his huge chest.

Sometimes when Otto leads us from room to room in the old house, he lowers his voice to a whisper. He talks so low, we can barely hear him. Then his tiny eyes will bulge. He'll point—and *scream*: "There's the ghost! There!"

10

Stephanie and I always scream.

Even Otto's smile is scary.

Stephanie and I have taken the Hill House tour so often, we could probably be tour guides. We know all the creepy old rooms. All the places where ghosts have been spotted.

Real ghosts!

It's the kind of place we love.

Do you want to know the story of Hill House? Well, here's the story that Otto, Edna and the other guides tell:

Hill House is two hundred years old. And it's been haunted practically from the day the stones were gathered to build it.

A young sea captain built the house for his new bride. But the day the big house was finished, the captain was called out to sea.

His young wife moved into the huge house all alone. It was cold and dark, and the rooms and hallways seemed to stretch on for ever.

For months and months, she stared out of their bedroom window. The window that faced the river. Waiting patiently for the captain's return.

Winter passed. Then spring, then summer.

But he never came back.

The captain was lost at sea.

One year after the sea captain disappeared, a ghost appeared in the halls of Hill House. The ghost of the young sea captain. He had come back from the dead, back to find his wife.

Every night he floated through the long, twisting halls. He carried a lantern and called out his wife's name. "Annabel! Annabel!"

But Annabel never answered.

In her grief, she had fled from the old house. She never wanted to see it again.

Another family had moved in. As the years passed, many people heard the ghost's nightly calls. "Annabel! Annabel!" Through the twisting halls and cold rooms of the house.

"Annabel! Annabel!"

People heard the sad, frightening calls. But no one ever saw the ghost.

Then, one hundred years ago, a family named Craw bought the house. The Craws had a thirteen-year-old boy named Andrew.

Andrew was a nasty, mean-natured boy. He delighted in playing cruel tricks on the servants. He scared them out of their wits.

He once threw a cat out of a window. He was disappointed when it survived.

Even Andrew's own parents couldn't bear to spend time with the mean-tempered boy. He spent his days on his own, exploring the old mansion, looking for trouble he could get into.

One day he discovered a room he had never explored before. He pushed open the heavy wooden door. It let out a loud creak.

Then he stepped inside.

A lantern glowed dimly on a small table. The boy saw no other furniture in the large room. No one at the table.

"How strange," he thought. "Why should I find a burning lantern in an empty room?"

Andrew approached the lantern. As he leaned down to lower the wick, the ghost appeared.

The sea captain!

Over the years, the ghost had grown into an old and terrifying creature. He had long, white fingernails that curled in spirals. Cracked, black teeth poked out from between swollen, dry lips. And a scraggly white beard hid the ghost's face from view.

The boy stared in horror. "Who—who are you?" he stammered.

The ghost didn't utter a word. He floated in the yellow lantern light, glaring hard at the boy.

"Who are you? What do you want? Why are you here?" the boy demanded.

When the ghost still didn't reply, Andrew turned—and tried to run.

But before he had moved two steps, he felt the ghost's cold breath on his neck.

Andrew grabbed for the door. But the old ghost swirled around him, swirled darkly, a swirl of black smoke in the dim yellow light.

"No! Stop!" the boy screamed. "Let me go!"

The ghost's mouth gaped open, revealing a

bottomless black hole. Finally, it spoke—in a whisper that sounded like the scratch of dead leaves. "Now that you have seen me, you cannot leave."

"No!" The boy shrieked. "Let me go! Let me go!"

The ghost ignored the boy's cries. He repeated his dry, cold words: "Now that you have seen me, you cannot leave."

The old ghost raised his hands to the boy's head. His icy fingers spread over Andrew's face. The hands tightened. Tightened.

Do you know what happened next?

The ghost pulled off the boy's head—and hid it somewhere in the house!

After hiding the head, hiding it away in the huge, dark mansion, the ghost of the sea captain let out a final howl that made the heavy stone walls tremble.

The terrifying howl ended with the cry, "Annabel! Annabel!"

Then the old ghost disappeared for ever.

But Hill House was not freed from ghosts. A new ghost now haunted the endless, twisting halls.

From then on, Andrew haunted Hill House. Every night the ghost of the poor boy searched the halls and rooms, looking for his missing head.

All through the house (say Otto and the other tour guides) you can hear the footsteps of the Headless Ghost, searching, always searching.

And each room of the house now has a terrifying story of its own.

Are the stories true?

Well, Stephanie and I believe them. That's why we take the tour so often.

We must have explored the old place at least a hundred times.

Hill House is such awesome fun.

At least it *was* fun—until Stephanie had another one of her bright ideas.

After Stephanie's bright idea, Hill House wasn't fun any more.

Hill House became a truly scary place.

The trouble started a few weeks ago when Stephanie suddenly got bored.

It was about ten o'clock at night. We were out haunting the neighbourhood. We did our terrifying wolf howl outside Geena Jeffers' window. Then we went next door to Terri Abel's house. We put some chicken bones in her letterbox—just because it's creepy to reach in your letterbox and feel bones.

Then we crept across the street to Ben Fuller's house.

Ben was our last stop for the night. Ben is a kid in our class, and we have a special scare for him.

You see, he's afraid of bugs, which makes him really easy to scare.

Even though it's pretty cold out, he sleeps with his bedroom window open. So Stephanie and I like to step up to his window and toss rubber spiders on to Ben as he sleeps.

The rubber spiders tickle his face. He wakes up. And starts to scream.

Every time.

He always thinks the spiders are real.

He screams and tries to scramble out of bed. He gets all tangled in his covers and *thuds* on to the floor.

Then Stephanie and I congratulate each other on a job well done. And we go home to bed.

But tonight, as we tossed the rubber spiders at Ben's sleeping face, Stephanie turned to me and whispered, "I just had a great idea."

"Huh?" I started to reply. But Ben's scream interrupted me.

We listened to him scream, then *thud* to the floor.

Stephanie and I slapped each other a high five. Then we took off, running across the dark back gardens, our trainers thumping the hard, nearly-frozen ground.

We stopped in front of the split oak tree in my front garden. The tree trunk is completely split in two. But Dad doesn't have the heart to have the tree taken away.

"What is your great idea?" I asked Stephanie breathlessly.

Her dark eyes flashed. "I've been thinking. Every time we go out to haunt the neighbourhood, we scare the same old kids. It's starting to get boring."

I wasn't bored. But I knew that once Stephanie gets an idea, there's no stopping her. "So, do you want to find some new kids to scare?" I asked.

"No. Not new kids. Something else." She began to walk around the tree. Circling it. "We need a new challenge."

"Like what?" I asked.

"Our scares are all kids' stuff," she complained. "We make some spooky sounds, toss a few things inside an open window—and everyone is frightened to death. It's too easy."

"Yeah," I agreed. "But it's funny."

She ignored me. She stuck her head through the split in the tree trunk. "Duane, what's the scariest place in Wheeler Falls?"

That was easy. "Hill House, of course," I answered.

"Right. And what makes it so scary?"

"All the ghost stories. But especially the one about the boy searching for his head."

"Yes!" Stephanie cried. All I could see now was her head, poking through the split oak tree. "The Headless Ghost!" she cried in a deep voice, and let out a long, scary laugh.

"What's your problem?" I demanded. "Are you trying to haunt *me* now?"

Her head seemed to float in the darkness. "We need to haunt Hill House," she declared in a whisper.

19

"Excuse me?" I cried. "Stephanie, what are you talking about?"

"We'll take the Hill House tour and sneak off on our own," Stephanie replied thoughtfully.

I shook my head. "Give me a break. Why would we do that?"

Stephanie's face seemed to glow, floating by itself in the tree trunk. "We'll sneak off on our own—to search for the ghost's head."

I stared back at her. "You're kidding, right?"

I walked behind the tree and tugged her away from it. The floating head trick was starting to give me the creeps.

"No, Duane, I'm not kidding," she replied, shoving me away. "We need a challenge. We need something new. Prowling around the neighbourhood, terrifying everyone we know— that's just kids' stuff. Bor-ing."

"But you don't believe the story about the missing head—do you?" I protested. "It's just a ghost story. We can search and search. But there *is* no head. It's all a story they made up for the tourists."

Stephanie narrowed her eyes at me. "I think you're scared, Duane."

"Huh? Me?" My voice got pretty shrill.

A cloud rolled over the moon, making my front garden even darker. A chill ran down my back. I pulled my jacket around me tighter.

"I'm not afraid to sneak off from the tour and search Hill House on our own," I told Stephanie. "I just think it's a big waste of time."

"Duane, you're shivering," she teased. "Shivering with fright."

"I am not!" I screamed. "Come on. Let's go to Hill House. Right now. I'll show you.'

A grin spread over Stephanie's face. She tossed back her head and let out a long howl. A victory howl. "This is going to be the coolest thing the Twin Terrors have ever done!" she cried, slapping me a high five that made my hand sting.

She dragged me up Hill Street. The whole way there, I didn't say one word. Was I afraid?

Maybe a little.

We climbed the steep, weed-choked hill and stood before the front steps of Hill House. The old house looked even bigger at night. Three storeys tall. With turrets and balconies and dozens of windows, all dark and shuttered.

All the houses in our neighbourhood are brick or clapboard. Hill House is the only one made out of stone slabs. Dark grey slabs.

I always have to hold my breath when I stand close to Hill House. The stone is covered with a blanket of thick green moss. Two hundred years of it. Putrid, mouldy moss that doesn't exactly smell like a flower garden.

I peered up. Up at the round turret that stretched to the purple sky. A gargoyle, carved in stone, perched at the very top. It grinned down at us, as if challenging us to go inside.

My knees suddenly felt weak.

The house stood in total darkness, except for a single candle over the front doorway. But the tours were still going on. The last tour left at ten-thirty every night. The guides said the late tours were the best—the best time to see a ghost.

I read the sign etched in stone beside the door. ENTER HILL HOUSE—AND YOUR LIFE WILL BE CHANGED, FOR EVER.

I'd read that sign a hundred times. I always thought it was funny—in a corny sort of way.

But tonight it gave me the creeps.

Tonight was going to be different.

"Come on," Stephanie said, pulling me by the hand. "We're just in time for the next tour."

The candle flickered. The heavy wooden door

swung open. By itself. I don't know how, but it always does that.

"Well, are you coming or not?" Stephanie demanded, stepping into the dark entryway.

"Coming," I gulped.

Otto met us as we stepped inside the door. Otto always reminds me of an enormous dolphin. He has a big, smooth bald head. And he's sort of shaped like a dolphin. He must weigh about sixty kilos!

Otto was dressed entirely in black, as always. Black shirt. Black trousers. Black socks. Black shoes. And gloves—you guessed it—black. It's the uniform that all the tour guides wear.

"Look who's here!" he called. "Stephanie and Duane!" He broke out into a wide grin. His tiny eyes flashed in the candlelight.

"Our favourite guide!" Stephanie greeted him. "Are we in time for the next tour?"

We pushed through the turnstile without paying. We're such regulars at Hill House that they don't even charge us any more.

"About five minutes, guys," Otto told us. "You two are out late tonight, huh?"

"Yeah ... well," Stephanie hesitated. "It's

more fun to take the tour at night. Isn't it, Duane?" She jabbed my side.

"You can say that again," I mumbled.

We moved into the front hall with some others who were waiting for the tour to begin. Teenagers mostly, out on dates.

The front hall is bigger than my living room and dining room put together. And except for the winding staircase in the centre, it's completely bare. No furniture at all.

Shadows swept across the floor. I gazed around the room. No electric lights. Small torches were hung from the peeling, cracked walls. The orange torchlight flickered and bent.

In the dancing light, I counted the people around me. Nine of them. Stephanie and I were the only kids.

Otto lit a lantern and crossed to the front of the hall. He held it up high and cleared his throat.

Stephanie and I grinned at each other. Otto always starts the tour the same way. He thinks the lantern adds atmosphere.

"Ladies and gentlemen," he boomed. "Welcome to Hill House. We hope you will survive your tour tonight." Then he gave a low, evil laugh.

Stephanie and I mouthed Otto's next words along with him:

"In 1795, a prosperous sea captain, William

P. Bell, built himself a home on the highest hill in Wheeler Falls. It was the finest home ever built here at the time—three storeys high, nine fireplaces and over thirty rooms.

"Captain Bell spared no expense. Why? Because he hoped to retire here and finish his days in splendour with his young and beautiful wife. But it was not to be."

Otto cackled, and so did Stephanie and I. We knew every move Otto had.

Otto went on. "Captain Bell died at sea in a terrible shipwreck—before he ever had a chance to live in his beautiful house. His young bride, Annabel, fled the house in horror and sorrow."

Now Otto's voice dropped. "But soon after Annabel left, strange things began to happen in Hill House."

This was Otto's cue to start walking towards the winding stairs. The old, wooden staircase is narrow and creaky. When Otto starts to climb, the stairs groan and grumble beneath him as if in pain.

Keeping silent, we followed Otto up the stairs to the first floor. Stephanie and I love this part, because Otto doesn't say a word the whole time. He just huffs along in the darkness while everyone tries to keep up with him.

He starts talking again when he reaches Captain Bell's bedroom. A big, wood-panelled room with a fireplace and a view of the river.

"Soon after Captain Bell's widow ran away," Otto reported, "people in Wheeler Falls began reporting strange sightings. Sightings of a man who resembled Captain Bell. He was always seen here, standing by his window, holding his lantern aloft."

Otto moved to the window and raised his lantern. "On a windless night, if you listened carefully, you could sometimes hear him calling out her name in a low, mournful voice."

Otto took a deep breath, then called softly: "Annabel. Annabel. Annabel. . ."

Otto swung the lantern back and forth for effect. By now, he had everyone's complete attention.

"But of course, there's more," he whispered.

As we followed him through the upstairs rooms, Otto told us how Captain Bell haunted the house for about a hundred years. "People who moved into Hill House tried all kinds of ways to get rid of the ghost. But it was determined to stay."

Then Otto told everyone about the boy finding the ghost and getting his head pulled off. "The ghost of the sea captain vanished. The headless ghost of the boy continued to haunt the house. But that wasn't the end of it."

Into the long, dark hallway now. Torches darting and flickering along the walls. "Tragedy continued to haunt Hill House," Otto continued. "Shortly after young Andrew Craw's death, his twelve-year-old sister Hannah went mad. Let's go to her room next."

He led us down the hall to Hannah's room.

Stephanie loves Hannah's room. Hannah collected porcelain dolls. And she had hundreds of them. All with the same long yellow hair, painted rosy cheeks and blue-tinted eyelids.

"After her brother was killed, Hannah went crazy," Otto told us all in a hushed voice. "All day long, for eighty years, she sat in her rocking chair over there in the corner. And she played with her dolls. She never left her room. Ever."

He pointed to a worn rocking chair. "Hannah died there. An old lady surrounded by her dolls."

The floorboards creaked under him as Otto crossed the room. Setting the lantern down, he lowered his big body into the rocking chair.

The chair made a cracking sound. I always think Otto is going to crush it! He started to rock. Slowly. The chair groaned with each move. We all watched him in silence.

"Some people swear that poor Hannah is still here," he said softly. "They say they've seen a young girl sitting in this chair, combing a doll's hair."

He rocked slowly, letting the idea sink in. "And then we come to the story of Hannah's mother."

With a grunt, Otto pulled himself to his feet. He grabbed up the lantern and made his way to the top of the long, dark stairway at the end of the hall.

"Soon after her son's tragedy, the mother met her own terrible fate. She was on her way down these stairs one night when she tripped and fell to her death."

Otto gazed down the stairs and shook his head sadly.

He does this every time. As I said, Stephanie and I know his every move.

But we hadn't come here tonight to watch Otto perform. I knew that sooner or later, Stephanie would want to get going. So I started glancing around. To see if it was a good time for us to sneak away from the others.

And that's when I saw the strange kid. Watching us.

I hadn't seen him when we first came in. In fact, I'm sure he wasn't there when the tour started. I had counted nine people. No kids.

The boy was about our age, with wavy blond hair and pale skin. Very pale skin. He was wearing black jeans and a black turtleneck that made his face look even whiter.

I edged over to Stephanie. She was hanging back from the group.

"You ready?" she whispered.

Otto had started back down the stairs. If we were going to sneak away from the tour, now was the time.

But I could see that weird kid still staring at us.

Staring hard.

He was giving me the creeps.

"We can't go. Someone's watching us," I whispered to Stephanie.

"Who?"

"That weird kid over there." I motioned with my eyes.

He was still staring at us. He didn't even try to be polite and turn away when we caught him.

Why was he watching us like that? What was his *problem*?

Something told me we should wait. Something told me not to hide from the others just yet.

But Stephanie had other ideas. "Forget him," she said. "He's nobody." She grabbed my arm— and tugged. "Let's go!"

We pressed against the cold wall of the hallway and watched the others follow Otto down the stairs.

I held my breath until I heard the last footsteps leave the stairway. We were alone now. Alone in the long, dark hall.

I turned to Stephanie. I could barely see her face. "Now what?" I asked.

"Now we do some exploring on our own!" Stephanie declared, rubbing her hands together. "This is so exciting!"

I gazed down the long hallway. I didn't feel very excited. I felt kind of scared.

I heard a low groan from a room across the hall. The ceiling creaked above our heads. The wind rattled the windows in the room we had just come from.

"Steph—are you sure—?" I started.

But she was already hurrying down the hall, walking on tiptoes to keep the floors from squeaking. "Come on, Duane. Let's search for the ghost's head," she whispered back to me, her dark hair flying behind her. "Who knows? We might find it."

"Yeah. Sure." I rolled my eyes.

I didn't think the chances were too good. How do you find a hundred-year-old head? And what if you *do* find it?

Yuck!

What would it look like? Just a skull?

I followed Stephanie down the hall. But I really didn't want to be there. I like haunting the neighbourhood and scaring other people.

I don't like scaring myself!

Stephanie led the way into a bedroom we had seen on other tours. It was called the Green Room. Because the wallpaper was decorated with green vines. Tangle after tangle of green vines. Up and down the walls and across the ceiling, too.

How could anyone sleep in here? I wondered. It was like being trapped in a thick jungle.

We both stopped inside the doorway and stared at the tangles of vines on all sides of us. Stephanie and I call the Green Room by another name. The Scratching Room.

Otto once told us that something terrible happened here sixty years ago. The two guests who stayed in the room woke up with a disgusting purple rash.

The rash started on their hands and arms. It spread to their faces. Then it spread over their whole bodies.

Big purple sores that itched like crazy.

Doctors from all around the world were called to study the rash. They couldn't figure out what it was. And they couldn't figure out how to cure it.

Something in the Green Room caused the rash.

But no one ever figured out what it was.

That's the story Otto and the other guides tell. It might be true. All the weird, scary stories Otto tells might be true. Who knows?

"Come on, Duane!" Stephanie prodded. "Let's look for the head. We don't have much time before Otto sees that we're missing."

She trotted across the room and dived under the bed.

"Steph—please!" I started. I stepped carefully over to the low, wooden dressing-table in the corner.

"We're not going to find a ghost's head in here. Let's go," I pleaded.

She couldn't hear me. She had climbed under the bed.

"Steph—?"

After a few seconds, she backed out. As she turned towards me, I saw that her face was bright red.

"Duane!" she cried. "I. . . I. . ."

Her dark eyes bulged. Her mouth dropped open in horror. She grabbed the sides of her face.

"What is it? What's wrong?" I cried, stumbling across the room towards her.

"Ohhh, it itches! It itches so badly!" Stephanie wailed.

I started to cry out. But my voice got caught in my throat.

Stephanie began to rub her face. She frantically rubbed her cheeks, her forehead, her chin.

"Owwww. It itches! It really itches!" She started to scratch her scalp with both hands.

I grabbed her arm and tried to pull her up from the floor. "The rash! Let's get you home!" I cried. "Come on! Your parents will get the doctor! And. . . and. . ."

I stopped when I saw that she was laughing.

I dropped her arm and stepped back.

She stood up, straightening her hair. "Duane, you idiot," she muttered. "Are you going to fall for every stupid joke tonight!"

"No way!" I replied angrily. "I just thought—"

She gave me a shove. "You're too easy to scare. How could you fall for such a stupid joke?"

I shoved her back. "Just don't pull any more silly jokes, okay?" I snarled. "I mean it, Stephanie. I don't think it's funny. I really don't. I'm not going to fall for any more stupid jokes. So don't even try."

She wasn't listening to me. She was staring over my shoulder. Staring in open-mouthed shock.

"Oh, I d-don't *believe* it!" she stammered. "There it is! There's the head!"

I fell for it again.

I couldn't help myself.

I let out a shrill scream.

I spun around so hard, I nearly knocked myself over. I followed Stephanie's finger. I squinted hard in the direction she pointed.

She was pointing to a grey clump of dust.

"Sucker! Sucker!" She slapped me on the back and started to giggle.

I uttered a low growl and balled my hands into tight fists. But I didn't say anything. I could feel my face burning. I knew that I was blushing.

"You're too easy to scare, Duane," Stephanie teased again. "Admit it."

"Let's just get back to the tour," I grumbled.

"No way, Duane. This is fun. Let's try the next room. Come on."

When she saw that I wasn't following her,

she said, "I won't scare you like that any more. Promise."

I saw that her fingers were crossed. But I followed her anyway.

What choice did I have?

We crept through the narrow hall that connected us to the next room. And found ourselves in Andrew's room. Poor, headless Andrew.

It still had all his old stuff in it. Games and toys from a hundred years ago. An old-fashioned wooden bicycle leaning against one wall.

Everything just the way it was. Before Andrew met up with the sea captain's ghost.

A lantern on the dressing-table cast blue shadows on the walls. I didn't know if I believed the ghost story or not. But something told me that if Andrew's head were anywhere, we'd find it here. In his room.

Under his old-fashioned-looking canopy bed. Or hidden under his dusty, faded toys.

Stephanie tiptoed over to the toys. She bent down and started to move things aside. Little wooden bowling pins. An old-fashioned board game, the colours all faded to brown. A set of metal toy soldiers.

"Check around the bed, Duane," she whispered.

I started across the room. "Steph, we shouldn't be touching this stuff. You know the tour guides never let us touch anything."

Stephanie set down an old wooden top. "Do you want to find the head or not?"

"You really think there's a ghost's head hidden in this house?"

"Duane, that's what we're here to find out— right?"

I sighed and stepped over to the bed. I could see there was no use arguing with Stephanie tonight.

I ducked my head under the purple canopy and studied the bed. A boy actually slept in this bed, I told myself.

Andrew actually slept under this quilt. A hundred years ago.

The thought gave me a chill.

I tried to picture a boy about my age sleeping in this heavy, old bed.

"Go ahead. Check out the bed," Stephanie instructed from across the room.

I leaned over and patted the grey and brown patchwork quilt. It felt cold and smooth.

I punched the pillows. They felt soft and feathery. Nothing hidden inside the pillow cases.

I was about to test the mattress when the quilt began to move.

It rustled over the sheets. A soft, scratchy sound.

Then, as I stared in horror, the grey and brown quilt began to slide down the bed.

There was no one in the bed. No one!

But someone was pushing the quilt down, down to the bottom of the bed.

I swallowed a scream.

"You've got to move faster, Duane," Stephanie said.

I turned and saw her standing at the end of the bed. Holding the bottom of the quilt in both hands.

"We don't have all night!" she declared. She pulled the quilt down further. "Nothing in the bed. Come on. Let's move on."

A sigh escaped my lips. Stephanie had tugged down the quilt and scared me again.

No ghost in the bed. No ghost pushing down the covers to climb out and grab me.

Only Stephanie.

At least this time she hadn't seen how frightened I was.

We worked together to pull the quilt back into place. She smiled at me. "This is great fun," she said.

"For sure," I agreed. I hoped she couldn't see

that I was still shaking. "It's a lot more fun than tossing rubber spiders into Ben Fuller's bedroom window."

"I like being in this house so late at night. I like sneaking off from the group. I can feel a ghost lurking nearby," Stephanie whispered.

"You c-can?" I stammered, glancing quickly around the room.

My eyes stopped at the bottom of the door to the hallway.

There it sat. On the floor. Wedged between the door and the wall. Half-hidden in deep shadow.

The head.

This time, I saw the head.

Not a joke. Not a cruel trick.

Through the grey-black shadows, I saw the round skull. And I saw the two black eye sockets. Empty eye sockets. Two dark holes in the skull.

Staring up at me.

Staring.

I grabbed Stephanie's arm. I started to panic.

But there was no need.

Stephanie had seen it, too.

I was the first to move. I took a step towards the door. Then another.

I heard sharp gasps. Someone breathing hard. Close behind me.

It took me a few seconds to realize it was Stephanie.

Keeping my eyes on the head, I made my way into the dark corner. My heart started to pound as I bent down and reached for it with both hands.

The black eye sockets stared up at me. Round, sad eyes.

My hands trembled.

I started to scoop it up.

But it slipped out of my hands. And started to roll away.

Stephanie let out a cry as the head rolled over the floor towards her.

In the orange light from the lantern, I saw her frightened expression. I saw that she was frozen there.

The head rolled over the floor and bumped against her trainer. It came to a stop inches in front of her.

The empty black eye sockets stared up at her.

"Duane—" she called, staring down at it, hands pressed against her cheeks. "I didn't think—I didn't really think we'd find it. I—I—"

I hurried back across the room. It's my turn to be the brave one, I decided. My turn to show Stephanie that I'm not a wimp who's afraid of every shadow.

My turn to show Stephanie.

I scooped up the ghost's head in both hands. I raised it in front of Stephanie. Then I moved towards the lantern on the dressing-table.

The head felt hard. Smoother than I thought.

The eye sockets were deep.

Stephanie stayed close by my side. Together we made our way into the orange lantern light.

I let out a groan when I realized I wasn't carrying a ghost's head.

Stephanie groaned too when she saw what I held in my hands.

A bowling ball.

I was carrying an old wooden bowling ball, the pale wood cracked and chipped.

"I don't believe it," Stephanie murmured, slapping her forehead.

My eyes went to the wooden bowling pins, lying among Andrew's old toys. "This must be the ball that went with those pins," I said softly.

Stephanie grabbed it from me and turned it between her hands. "But it only has two holes."

I nodded. "Yeah. In those days, bowling balls only had two holes. My dad told me about it one day when we went bowling. Dad never could figure out what they did with their thumb."

Stephanie stuck her fingers into the two holes. The "eye-sockets". She shook her head. I could see she was really disappointed.

We could hear Otto's voice, booming from somewhere downstairs.

Stephanie sighed. "Maybe we should go down

44

and rejoin the tour," she suggested. She rolled the ball back to the pile of toys.

"No way!" I exclaimed.

I liked being the brave one for a change. I didn't want to quit while I was ahead.

"It's getting kind of late," Stephanie said. "And we're not going to find any ghost head up here."

"That's because we've already explored these rooms a hundred times," I told her. "I think we should find a room we've never explored before."

She scrunched up her face, thinking hard. "Duane, do you mean—?"

"I mean, the ghost head is probably hidden in a room the tour doesn't go through. Maybe upstairs. You know. On the top floor."

Stephanie's eyes grew wide. "You want to sneak up to the top floor?"

I nodded. "Why not? That's probably where all the ghosts hang out—right?"

She studied me, her eyes searching mine. I knew she was surprised by my brave idea.

Of course, I didn't feel very brave at all. I just wanted to impress her. I just wanted to be the brave one for a change.

I was hoping that she'd say no. I was hoping she'd say, "Let's go back downstairs, Duane."

But instead, an excited grin spread over her face. And she said, "Okay. Let's do it!"

So I was stuck being the brave one.

We both had to be brave now. The Twin Terrors, on their way up the dark, creaking stairway that led to the third floor.

A sign beside the stairs read: NO VISITORS.

We stepped right past it and began climbing the narrow staircase. Side by side.

I couldn't hear Otto's voice any more. Now I could only hear the creak and squeak of the steps beneath our trainers. And the steady *thud thud thud* of my heart.

The air grew hot and damp as we reached the top. I squinted down a long, dark hallway. There were no lanterns. No candles.

The only light came from the window at the end of the hall. Pale light from outside that cast everything in an eerie, ghostly blue.

"Let's start in the first room," Stephanie

suggested, whispering. She brushed her dark hair off her face.

It was so hot up here, I had sweat running down my forehead. I mopped it up with my jacket sleeve and followed Stephanie to the first room on the right.

The heavy wooden door was half open. We slid in through the opening. Pale blue light washed in through the dust-caked windows.

I waited for my eyes to adjust. Then I squinted around the large room.

Empty. Completely empty. No furniture. No sign of life.

Or ghosts.

"Steph—look." I pointed to a narrow door against the far wall. "Let's check it out."

We crept across the bare floor. Through the dusty window, I glimpsed the full moon, high over the bare trees now.

The doorway led to another room. Smaller and even warmer. A steam radiator clanked against one wall. Two old-fashioned-looking sofas stood facing each other in the centre of the room. No other furniture.

"Let's keep moving," Stephanie whispered.

Another narrow door led to another dark room. "The rooms up here are all connected," I murmured. I sneezed. Sneezed again.

"Ssshhh. Quiet, Duane," Stephanie scolded. "The ghosts will hear us coming."

47

"I can't help it," I protested. "It's so dusty up here."

We were in some kind of sewing room. An old sewing machine stood on a table in front of the window. A box at my feet was filled with balls of black wool.

I bent down and pawed quickly through the balls of wool. No head hidden in there.

We had stepped into the next room before we realized it was completely dark.

The window was partly shuttered. Only a tiny square of grey light crept through from outside.

"I-I can't see anything," Stephanie declared. I felt her hand grasp my arm. "It's too dark. Let's get out of here, Duane."

I started to reply. But a loud *thump* made my breath catch in my throat.

Stephanie's hand squeezed my hand. "Duane, did you make that *thump*?"

Another *thump*. Closer to us.

"No. Not m-me," I stammered.

Another *thump* on the floor.

"We're not alone in here," Stephanie whispered.

I took a deep breath. "Who is it?" I called. "Who's there?"

"Who's there?" I choked out.

Stephanie squeezed my arm so hard, it hurt. But I made no attempt to move away from her.

I heard soft footsteps. Ghostly footsteps.

A cold chill froze the back of my neck. I clamped my jaw shut to keep my teeth from chattering.

And then yellow eyes floated towards us through the thick darkness.

Four yellow eyes.

The creature had *four* eyes!

A gurgling sound escaped my throat. I couldn't breathe. I couldn't move.

I stared straight ahead. Listening.

Watching.

The eyes floated apart in pairs. Two eyes moved to the right, two to the left.

"Noooo!" I cried out when I saw more eyes.

Yellow eyes in the corners of the room. Evil eyes glinting at us from against the wall.

Yellow eyes all along the floor.

Yellow eyes all around us.

Cat-like yellow eyes glaring in silence at Stephanie and me as we huddled together in the centre of the room.

Cat-like eyes.

Cats' eyes.

Because the room was filled with cats.

A shrill *yowl* gave them away. A long *meeeeyoww* from the windowsill made Stephanie and me both sigh in relief.

A cat brushed against my leg. Startled, I jumped aside, bumping into Stephanie.

She bumped me back.

More cats meowed. Another cat brushed the back of my jeans leg.

"I-I think these cats are lonely," Stephanie stammered. "Do you think anyone ever comes up here?"

"I don't care," I snapped. "All these yellow eyes floating around. I thought. . . I thought. . . Well. . . I don't know *what* I thought! It's creepy. Let's get out of here."

For once, Stephanie didn't argue.

She led the way to the door at the back of the room. All around us, cats were howling and yowling.

Another one brushed my leg.

Stephanie tripped over a cat. In the darkness, I saw her fall. She landed on her knees with a hard *thud*.

The cats all began to screech.

"Are you okay?" I cried, hurrying to help pull her up.

The cats were howling so loud, I couldn't hear her reply.

We jogged to the door, pulled it open, and escaped.

I closed the door behind us. Silence now. "Where are we?" I whispered.

"I-I don't know," Stephanie stammered, keeping close to the wall.

I moved to a tall, narrow window and peered through the dusty glass. The window led out to a small balcony. The balcony jutted out from the grey shingled roof.

Pale white moonlight washed in through the window.

I turned back to Stephanie. "We're in some kind of back hallway," I guessed. The long, narrow hallway seemed to stretch on for ever. "Maybe these rooms are used by the workers. You know. Manny, the night watchman. The house cleaners. And the tour guides."

Stephanie sighed. She stared down the long hallway. "Let's go downstairs and find Otto and the tour group. I think we've done enough exploring for tonight."

51

I agreed. "There must be stairs at the end of this hall. Let's go."

I took four or five steps. Then I felt the ghostly hands.

They brushed over my face. My neck. My body.

Sticky, dry, invisible hands.

The hands pushed me back as they clung to my skin.

'Ohhhh, help!' Stephanie moaned.

The ghosts had her in their grasp, too.

The ghost's filmy hands brushed over me. I could feel the soft fingers—dry and soft as air—tighten around my skin.

Stephanie's hands thrashed wildly. Beside me in the dark hall, she struggled to free herself.

"It-it's like a net!" she choked out.

I swiped at my face. My hair.

I spun away. But the dry fingers clung to me. Tightening. Tightening.

And I realized we hadn't walked into a ghost's grasp.

Tugging and tearing frantically with both hands, I realized we had walked into cobwebs.

A thick curtain of cobwebs.

The blanket of sticky threads had fallen over us like a fisherman's net. The more we struggled, the tighter it wrapped itself around us.

"Stephanie—it's *cobwebs*!" I cried. I tugged a thick, stringy wad of them off my face.

53

"Of course it's cobwebs!" she shot back, squirming and thrashing. "What did *you* think it was?"

"Uh . . . a ghost," I muttered.

Stephanie sniggered. "Duane, I know you have a good imagination. But if you start seeing ghosts *everywhere*, we'll never get out of here."

"I . . . I . . . I . . ." I didn't know what to say.

Stephanie had thought the same thing I did. She thought she'd been grabbed by a ghost. But now she was pretending she knew all along.

We stood there in the darkness, tearing the sticky threads off our faces and arms and bodies. I let out an angry groan. I couldn't brush the stuff from my hair!

"I'm going to itch *for ever*!" I wailed.

"I've got more bad news for you," Stephanie murmured.

I pulled a thick wad off my ear. "Huh?"

"Who do you think made these cobwebs?"

I didn't have to think about it. "Spiders?"

My arms and legs started to tingle. My back began to itch. I felt a light tingling on the back of my neck.

Were there spiders crawling up and down my body? Hundreds and hundreds of them?

Forgetting the wispy strings of cobweb, I started to run. Stephanie had the same idea. We both ran down the long hall, scratching and slapping at ourselves.

"Steph—the next time you have a great idea, *don't* have a great idea!" I warned her.

"Let's just get out of here!" she groaned.

We reached the end of the hall, still scratching as we ran.

No stairway.

How do we get back downstairs?

Another hall twisted to the left. Low candles over the doorways flickered and danced. Shadows darted over the worn carpet like slithering animals.

"Come on." I pulled Stephanie's arm. We had no choice. We had to follow this hallway, too.

We jogged side by side. The rooms were all dark and silent.

The candle flames dipped as we ran past. Our long shadows ran ahead of us, as if eager to get downstairs first.

I stopped when I heard someone laughing.

"Whoa," Stephanie murmured, breathing hard. Her dark eyes grew wide.

We both listened hard.

I heard voices. Inside the room at the end of the hall.

The door was closed. I couldn't make out the words. I heard a man say something. A woman laughed. Other people laughed.

"We've caught up with the tour," I whispered.

Stephanie scrunched up her face. "But the

tour never comes up here to the top floor," she protested.

We stepped up close to the door and listened again.

More laughter on the other side. A lot of people talking cheerfully, all at the same time. It sounded like a party.

I pressed my ear against the door. "I think the tour ended, and everyone is just chatting," I whispered.

Stephanie scratched the back of her neck. She pulled a stringy gob of cobweb from her hair. "Well, hurry, Duane. Open the door. Let's join them," she urged.

"I hope Otto doesn't ask us where we've been," I replied.

I grabbed the doorknob and pushed open the door.

Stephanie and I took a step inside.

And gasped in shock at what we saw.

The room stood empty.

Empty, silent and dark.

"What happened? Where is everyone?" Stephanie cried.

We took another step into the dark room. The floor creaked beneath us. The only sound.

"I don't get it," Stephanie whispered. "Didn't we just hear voices in here?"

"Lots," I said. "They were laughing and talking. It really sounded like a party."

"A big party," Stephanie added, her eyes darting around the empty room. "Tons of people."

A cold chill ran down the back of my neck. "I don't think we heard people," I whispered.

Stephanie turned to me. "Huh?"

"They weren't people," I croaked. "They were ghosts."

Her mouth dropped open. "And they all disappeared when we opened the door?"

I nodded. "I—I think I can still feel them in here. I can feel their presence."

Stephanie let out a frightened squeak. "Feel them? What do you mean?"

At that moment, a cold wind came whooshing through the room. It rushed over me, cold and dry. And it chilled me down to my toes.

Stephanie must have felt it, too. She wrapped her arms around her chest. "Brrr! Do you feel that breeze? Is the window open? How come it's so cold in here all of a sudden?" she asked.

She shivered again. Her voice became tiny. "We're not alone in here, are we?"

"I don't think so," I whispered. "I think we just crashed someone's party."

Stephanie and I stood there, feeling the cold of the room. I didn't dare move. Maybe a ghost was standing right beside me. Maybe the ghosts we heard were all around us, staring at us, preparing to swoop over us.

"Stephanie," I whispered. "What if we really have crashed their party? What if we've invaded the ghosts' quarters?"

Stephanie swallowed hard. She didn't reply.

Hadn't Andrew, the ghost boy, lost his head when he stumbled into the ghost's living quarters? Were we standing in the same living quarters? The same room where Andrew found the ghost of the old sea captain?

"Stephanie, I think we should get out of here," I said softly. "Now."

I wanted to run. I wanted to fly down the stairs. Fly out of Hill House. Fly to my safe, warm home where there were no ghosts.

No ghosts.

We spun around and bolted for the door.

Were the ghosts going to try to stop us?

No. We made it back into the flickering orange light of the hallway. I pulled the door shut behind us.

"The stairs. Where are the stairs?" Stephanie cried.

We stood at the end of the hall. Facing a solid wall. The flowers on the wallpaper appeared to open and close, moving in the darting candlelight.

I banged both fists against the wall. "How do we get out of here? How?"

Stephanie had already pulled open a door across the hall. I followed her inside.

"Oh, no!" Ghostly figures filled the room. It took me a few seconds to realize that I was staring at sheets pulled over furniture. Chairs and sofas covered with sheets.

"M-maybe this is the ghosts' living room," I stammered.

Stephanie didn't hear me. She had already burst through the open door against the far wall.

I followed her into another room, cluttered

with large crates. The crates were piled nearly to the ceiling.

Another room. Then another.

My heart began to pound. My throat ached.

I felt so discouraged. Were we ever going to find our way to the stairs?

Another door. Another dark, empty room.

"Hey, Steph—" I whispered. "I think we're going in circles."

Out into a long, twisting hallway. More candles. More flowers flickering darkly on the wallpaper.

We ran side by side down the hall. Until we came to a door I hadn't seen before. A door with a horseshoe nailed on to it.

Maybe it meant that our luck was about to change. I sure hoped so!

I grabbed the knob with a trembling hand. I pulled open the door.

A staircase!

"Yes!" I cried.

"Finally!" Stephanie gasped.

"This must be the servants' staircase," I guessed. "Maybe we've been in the servants' quarters all the time."

The stairway was blanketed in darkness. The stairs looked steep.

I took a step down, holding on to the wall. Then another step.

Stephanie had one hand on my shoulder.

When I stepped down, she stepped down, too.

Another step. Another. The soft *thuds* of our trainers echoed in the deep stairwell.

We had taken about ten steps when I heard footsteps.

Someone coming up the stairs.

Stephanie bumped me hard. I shot out both hands. Grabbed the wall to keep from falling down the stairs.

No time to turn and run.

The footsteps grew louder. And heavier. Light from an electric torch swept over Stephanie, then me.

Squinting against the light, I saw a dark figure climbing up to us. "So *there* you are!" his voice boomed, echoing in the stairwell.

A familiar voice.

"Otto!" Stephanie and I both cried.

He bounced up in front of us, moving the torch from her face to mine. "What are you two doing up here?" he demanded breathlessly.

"Uh . . . we got lost," I answered quickly.

"We got separated from the tour," Stephanie added. "We tried to find you."

"Yes. We tried," I chimed in. "We were

searching everywhere. But we couldn't catch up with the group."

Otto lowered the torch. I could see his tiny dark eyes narrowing at us. I don't think he believed our story.

"I thought you two knew my tour by heart," he said, rubbing his chin.

"We do," Stephanie insisted. "We lost our bearings. We got lost. And we—"

"But how did you get up here on the top floor?" Otto demanded.

"Well. . ." I started. But I couldn't think of a good answer. I turned back to Stephanie on the step above me.

"We heard voices up here. We thought it was you," she told Otto.

It wasn't exactly a lie. We *did* hear voices.

Otto lowered the beam of light to the stairs. "Well, let's get back downstairs. No one is allowed on this floor. It's private."

"Sorry," Stephanie and I murmured.

"Watch your step, kids," Otto warned. "These back stairs are very steep and rickety. I'll lead you back to the group. Edna took over for me while I went to find you."

Edna was our second-favourite tour guide. She was old and white-haired. Very pale and frail-looking, especially in her black tour-guide outfit.

But she was a great storyteller. With her

quivering, old voice, she really made you *believe* every frightening story she told you.

Stephanie and I eagerly clumped down the stairs, following Otto. His torch swept in front of us as he led us out on to the first floor. We followed a long hallway. A hallway I knew very well.

We stopped outside Joseph Craw's study. Joseph was Andrew's father. I peeked inside. A bright fire blazed in the fireplace.

Edna stood beside the fireplace, telling the tragic story of Joseph Craw to the tour group.

Stephanie and I had heard the sad story a hundred times. A year after Andrew had his head stolen, Joseph came home late one winter night. He took off his coat, then moved to the fireplace to warm himself.

No one knows how Joseph was burned up. At least, that's how Otto, Edna, and the other guides tell the story. Was he pushed into the fireplace? Did he fall in?

One guess is as good as another.

But when the maid came into the study the next morning, she found a horrifying sight.

She found two charred, blackened hands gripping the mantel.

Two hands, holding on tightly to the marble mantelpiece.

All that was left of Joseph Craw.

It's a yucky story—isn't it?

It gives me a chill every time I hear it.

As Otto led us to the study, Edna was just getting to the sickening part. The ending. "Do you want to rejoin the group?" Otto whispered.

"It's pretty late. I think we'd better get home," Stephanie told him.

I quickly agreed. "Thanks for rescuing us. We'll catch the tour again soon."

"Good night," Otto said, clicking off his torch. "You know the way out." He hurried into the study.

I started to leave. But stopped when I saw the boy again, the pale boy with the wavy blond hair. The boy in the black jeans and black turtleneck.

He stood away from the tour group. Close to the door. And he was staring at Stephanie and me again. Staring hard at us, a cold expression on his face.

"Come on," I whispered, grabbing Stephanie's arm. I tugged her away from the study door.

We quickly found the front stairway. A few seconds later, we pushed open the front door and stepped outside. A cold wind greeted us as we started down the hill. Wisps of black cloud floated like snakes over the moon.

"Well, that was fun!" Stephanie declared. She zipped her coat up to her chin.

"Fun?" I wasn't so sure. "It was kind of scary."

Stephanie grinned at me. "But we weren't afraid—right?"

I shivered. "Right."

"I'd like to go back and explore some more," she said. "You know. Maybe go back to that room with all the voices. Find some real ghosts."

"Yeah. Great," I agreed. I didn't feel like arguing with her. I felt pretty tired.

She pulled a wool scarf from her coat pocket. As she swung it around her neck, one end caught in a low pine bush.

"Hey—!" she cried out.

I moved to the bush and started to pull the scarf free.

And that's when I heard the voice.

Just a whisper. A whisper from the other side of the bush.

But I heard it very clearly.

"Did you find my head?"

That's what I heard.

"Did you find my head? Did you find it for me?"

I uttered a startled gasp and stared into the bush. "Stephanie— did you hear that?" I choked out.

No reply.

"Stephanie? Steph?"

I spun around. She was staring at me, her mouth open in surprise.

"Did you hear that whisper?" I asked again.

Then I realized she wasn't staring at me. She was staring past me.

I turned—and saw the strange, blond boy standing there beside the pine bush. "Hey—did you just whisper to us?" I demanded sharply.

He narrowed his pale grey eyes at me. "Huh? Me?"

"Yeah. You," I snapped. "Were you trying to scare us?"

He shook his head. "No way."

"You didn't whisper from behind this bush?" I asked again.

"I only just got out here," the boy insisted.

We saw him in Joseph Craw's study less than a minute ago, I told myself. How did he get out here so fast?

"Why did you follow us?" Stephanie demanded, shoving her scarf around her coat collar.

The boy shrugged.

"Why were you staring at us?" I asked, stepping up close to Stephanie.

The wind howled over the hilltop. The row of pine bushes shook in the gusty wind, as if shivering. Thin black clouds continued to snake their way over the pale moon.

The boy wore no coat. Only the black turtleneck and black jeans. The wind fluttered his long, wavy hair.

"We saw you staring at us," Stephanie repeated. "How come?"

He shrugged again. He kept his strange, grey eyes down at the ground. "I saw you sneak away," he said. "I wondered if . . . if you saw anything interesting."

"We got lost," I told him, glancing at Stephanie. "We didn't see much."

"What's your name?" Stephanie asked.

"Seth," he replied.

We told him our names.

"Do you live in Wheeler Falls?" Stephanie asked.

He shook his head. He kept his eyes down at his shoes. "No. I'm just visiting."

Why wouldn't he look us in the eye? Was he just shy?

"Are you sure you didn't whisper something from behind that bush?" I asked again.

He shook his head. "No way. Maybe someone was playing a joke on you."

"Maybe," I said. I stepped closer and kicked the bush. I don't know what I expected.

But nothing happened.

"You and Stephanie went exploring on your own?" Seth asked.

"Yeah. A little," I confessed. "We're kind of into ghosts."

When I said that, he jerked his head up. He raised his grey eyes and gazed hard at Stephanie, then at me.

His face had been a blank. No life to it. No expression at all.

But now I could see that he was really excited.

"Do you want to see some real ghosts?" he asked us, staring hard. "Do you?"

Seth stared at us as if challenging us. "Do you two want to see some real ghosts?"

"Yeah. Sure," Stephanie replied, returning his stare.

"What do you mean, Seth?" I demanded. "Have *you* ever seen a ghost?"

He nodded. "Yeah. In there." He pointed with his head, back to the big stone house.

"Huh?" I cried. "You saw a real ghost in Hill House? When?"

"Duane and I have taken the tour a hundred times," Stephanie told him. "We've never seen any ghost in there."

He sniggered. "Of course not. Do you think the ghosts come out when the tour group are in there? They wait till the house closes. They wait until all the tourists go home."

"How do *you* know?" I asked.

"I sneaked in," Seth replied. "Late one night."

"You *what*?" I cried. "How?"

"I found a door around the back. It was unlocked. I guess everyone forgot about it," Seth explained. "I sneaked in after the house was closed. And I—"

He stopped suddenly. His eyes were on the house.

I turned and saw the front door open. People stepped out, fastening their coats. The last tour had ended. People were heading for home.

"Over here!" Seth whispered.

We followed him behind the pine bushes and ducked down low. The people walked past us. They were laughing and talking about the house and all the ghost stories.

When they were down the hill, we stood up again. Seth brushed his long hair off his forehead. But the wind blew it right back.

"I sneaked in late at night, when the house was dark," he repeated.

"Your parents let you go out so late at night?" I asked.

A strange smile crossed his lips. "They didn't know," he said softly. The smile faded. "Your parents let you two out?"

Stephanie laughed. "Our parents don't know, either."

"Good," Seth replied.

"And you really saw a ghost?" I asked.

He nodded. Brushed his hair back again. "I

71

crept past Manny, the night watchman. He was sound asleep. Snoring away. I made my way to the front of the house. I was standing at the bottom of the big staircase—when I heard a laugh."

I gulped. "A laugh?"

"From the top of the stairs. I backed up against the wall. And I saw the ghost. A very old lady. In a long dress and a black bonnet. She wore a heavy black veil over the front of her face. But I could see her eyes through the veil. I could see them because they glowed bright red—like fire!"

"Wow!" Stephanie cried. "What did she do?"

Seth turned to the house. The front door had closed. The lantern over the door had been put out. The house stood in total darkness.

"The old ghost came sliding down the banister," he reported. "She tossed back her head—and screamed all the way down. And as she slid, her red eyes left a bright trail, like the tail of a comet."

"Weren't you scared?" I asked Seth. "Didn't you try to run away?"

"There was no time," he replied. "She came sliding down the banister, right towards me. Eyes blazing. Screaming like some kind of crazed animal. I was pressed against the wall. I couldn't move. And when she reached the bottom, I thought she'd grab me. But she vanished. Disappeared into the darkness. And all that was left was the faint red glow, floating in the air. The glow of her eyes."

"Oh, wow!" Stephanie cried.

"That's amazing!" I agreed.

"I want to sneak back in again," Seth declared, watching the house. "I'll bet there are more ghosts in there. I really want to see them."

"Me, too!" Stephanie cried eagerly.

Seth smiled at her. "So you'll come with me? Tomorrow night? I don't want to go back alone. It'll be so much more fun if you come, too."

The wind swirled sharply. The black clouds rolled over the moon, covering it, shutting out its light. The old house appeared to grow darker on its hilltop perch.

"So you'll come with me tomorrow night?" Seth asked again.

"Yeah. Great!" Stephanie told him. "I can't wait. How about you, Duane?" She turned to me. "You'll come, too—won't you. Duane? Won't you?"

21

I said yes.

I said I couldn't wait to see a real ghost.

I said I was shivering because of the cold wind. Not because I was scared.

We made a plan to meet at midnight tomorrow at the back of Hill House. Then Seth hurried away. And Stephanie and I walked home.

The street was dark and empty. Most of the house lights were out. Far in the distance, a dog howled.

Stephanie and I walked quickly, leaning into the wind. We usually didn't stay out this late.

Tomorrow night, we'd be even later.

"I don't trust that guy," I told Stephanie as we reached her front garden. "He's too weird."

I expected her to agree. But she said, "You're just jealous, Duane."

"Huh? Me? Jealous?" I couldn't believe she said that. "Why would I be jealous?"

"Because Seth is so brave. Because he saw a ghost and we didn't."

I shook my head. "Do you believe that crazy story about a ghost sliding down the banister? I think he made it up."

'Well," Stephanie replied thoughtfully, "we'll find out tomorrow night—won't we!"

Tomorrow night came too quickly.

I had a maths test in the afternoon. I don't think I did too well in it. I couldn't stop thinking about Seth, and Hill House and ghosts.

After dinner, Mum cornered me in the living room. She brushed back my hair and studied my face. "Why do you look so tired?" she asked. "You have dark circles around your eyes."

"Maybe I'm part raccoon," I replied. That's what I always say when she tells me I have circles around my eyes.

"I think you should go to bed early tonight," Dad chimed in. Dad always thinks that everyone should go to bed early.

So I went to my room at nine-thirty. But of course I didn't go to sleep.

I read a book and listened to a tape on my Walkman. And waited for Mum and Dad to go to bed. And watched the clock.

Mum and Dad are very heavy sleepers. You can pound and pound on their bedroom door, and they don't wake up. They once slept through a hurricane. That's the truth. They didn't hear the tree that fell on to our house!

Stephanie's parents are heavy sleepers, too. That's why it's so easy for the two of us to sneak out of our bedroom windows. That's why it's so easy for us to haunt our neighbourhood at night.

As the clock neared midnight, I wished we were going out on one of our usual haunting trips. I wished we were going to hide under Chrissy Jacob's window and howl like wolves. And then toss rubber spiders into Ben Fuller's bed.

But Stephanie had decided that was too boring.

We needed excitement. We needed to go ghost hunting. With a strange kid we'd never seen before.

At ten to twelve, I pulled on my down coat and crept out of my bedroom window. Another cold, windy night. I felt sprinkles of frozen rain on my forehead. So I pulled up my hood.

Stephanie was waiting for me at the bottom of her driveway. She had pulled her brown hair back in a ponytail. Her coat was open. She wore a heavy ski sweater underneath, pulled down over her jeans.

She raised her head and let out a ghostly howl. *"Owooooooo!"*

I clapped my hand over her open mouth. "You'll wake up the whole block!"

She laughed and backed away from me. "I'm a little excited. Aren't you?" She opened her mouth in another howl.

The frozen rain pattered on the ground. We hurried towards Hill House. The swirling wind scattered twigs and dead leaves as we walked. Most of the house lights had been turned off.

A car rolled by slowly as we turned on to Hill Street. Stephanie and I ducked behind a hedge. The driver might wonder why two kids were wandering around Wheeler Falls at midnight.

I wondered too.

We waited for the car to disappear. Then we continued our journey.

Our trainers crunched over the hard ground as we climbed the hill that led to the old haunted house. Hill House rose above us, like a silent monster waiting to swallow us up.

The last tour had ended. The lights were all off. Otto and Edna and the other tour guides were probably all home by now.

"Come on, Duane. Hurry," Stephanie urged. She started to run around the side of the house. "Seth is probably waiting."

"Wait up!" I cried. We followed a narrow dirt path around to the back.

Squinting into the darkness, I searched for Seth. No sign of him.

The back garden was cluttered with equipment of all kinds. A row of rusted metal rubbish bins formed a fence along one wall. A long wooden ladder lay on its side in the tall weeds. Wooden crates and barrels and cardboard boxes were strewn everywhere. A hand lawnmower tilted against the house.

"It—it's so much darker back here," Stephanie stammered. "Do you see Seth?"

"I can't see *anything*," I replied in a whisper. "Maybe he changed his mind. Maybe he isn't coming."

Stephanie started to reply. But a choked cry from the side of the house made us both jump.

I turned to see Seth stagger into view.

His blond hair was wild, flying around his face. His eyes bulged. His hands gripped his throat.

"The ghost!" he cried, stumbling clumsily. "The ghost—he—he *got* me!"

Then Seth collapsed at our feet and didn't move.

"Nice try, Seth," I said calmly.

"Nice fall," Stephanie added.

He raised his head slowly, staring up at us. "I didn't fool you?"

"No way," I replied.

Stephanie rolled her eyes. "That's Joke Number One," she told Seth. "Duane and I have pulled that one a thousand times."

Seth climbed to his feet and brushed off the front of his black turtleneck. He scowled, disappointed. "Just trying to give you a little scare."

"You'll have to do better than that," I told him.

"Duane and I are experts at giving scares," Stephanie added. "It's sort of our hobby."

Seth straightened his hair with both hands. "You two are weird," he murmured.

I brushed cold raindrops off my eyebrows. "Can we get inside?" I asked impatiently.

Seth led the way to the narrow door at the

far side of the house. "Did you two have any trouble sneaking out?" he asked, whispering.

"No. No trouble," Stephanie told him.

"Neither did I," he replied. He stepped up to the door and lifted the wooden latch. "I took the tour again tonight," he whispered. "Otto showed me some new things. Some new rooms we can explore."

"Great!" Stephanie exclaimed. "Do you promise we'll see a real ghost?"

Seth turned back to her. A strange smile spread over his face. "Promise," he said.

Seth gave the door a tug, and it creaked open.

We slipped inside. Into total blackness. Too dark to see where we were.

I took a few steps into the room—and bumped into Seth.

"Ssshhh," he warned. "Manny the night watchman is posted in the front rooms. He's probably asleep already. But we'd better stay in the back."

"Where are we?" I whispered.

"In one of the back rooms," Seth whispered. "Wait a few seconds. Our eyes will adjust."

"Can't we turn on a light?" I asked.

"Ghosts won't come out in the light," Seth replied.

We had closed the door behind us. But a cold wind still blew at my back.

I shivered.

A soft rattling sound made my breath catch in my throat.

Was I starting to hear things?

I pulled off my hood to hear better.

Silence now.

"I think I know where I can find some candles," Seth whispered. "You two wait here. Don't move."

"D-don't worry," I stammered. I didn't plan to go anywhere until I could see!

I heard Seth move away, making soft, scraping footsteps over the floor, keeping as quiet as he could. His footsteps faded into silence.

Then I felt another rush of cold wind against the back of my neck.

"Oh!" I cried out when I heard the rattling again.

A gentle rattling. Like the rattling of bones.

Another cold gust of wind swept over me. A ghost's cold breath, I thought. My whole body shook as a chill ran down my back.

I heard the rattling bones again. Louder. A clattering sound. So close.

I reached out in the thick blackness. Tried to grab on to the wall. Or a table. Or anything.

By my hands grabbed only air.

I swallowed hard. Calm down, Duane, I ordered myself. Seth will be back in a moment with some candles. Then you'll see that everything is okay.

82

But another jangle and clatter of bones made me gasp.

"Steph—did you hear that?" I whispered.

No reply.

A cold wind tingled my neck.

The bones rattled again.

"Steph? Do you hear that noise too? Steph?"

No reply.

"Stephanie? Steph?" I called.

She was gone.

Panic time.

My breaths came short and fast. My heart clattered louder than the skeleton bones. My whole body began to shake.

"Stephanie? Steph? Where *are* you?" I choked out weakly.

Then I saw the two yellow eyes moving towards me. Two glowing eyes, floating silently, gleaming with evil. Coming nearer. Nearer.

I froze.

I couldn't move. I couldn't see anything but those two gleaming, yellow eyes.

'Ohh!" I uttered a moan as they floated closer. And I could see them more clearly. See that they were candle flames.

Two candle flames, moving side by side.

In the soft yellow light, I saw Seth's face. And Stephanie's. They each carried a lighted candle in front of them.

"Stephanie—where *were* you?" I cried in a choked whisper. "I—I thought—"

"I went with Seth," she replied calmly.

The orange glow from her candle washed over me. I guess Stephanie could see how panicked I was. "I'm sorry, Duane," she said softly. "I said I was going with Seth. I thought you heard me."

"S-something is rattling," I stammered. "Bones, I think. I keep feeling a cold wind, and I keep hearing—"

Seth handed me a candle. "Light it," he instructed. "We'll look around. See what's rattling."

I took the candle and raised it to his. But my hand was shaking so badly, it took me five tries to light the wick. Finally, the candle flamed to life.

I gazed around in the flickering orange light.

"Hey—we're in the kitchen," Stephanie whispered.

A gust of cold wind blew past me. "Did you feel that?" I cried.

Seth pointed his candle flame towards the kitchen window. "Look, Duane—that window-pane. It's missing. The cold air is blowing in through the hole."

"Oh. Right."

Another blast of air. And then the rattling.

"Did you hear it?" I demanded.

Stephanie giggled. She pointed to the kitchen

wall. In the dim light, I saw big pots and pans hanging on the wall. "The wind is making them rattle," Stephanie explained.

"Ha-ha." I uttered a feeble laugh. "I knew that. I was just trying to scare you," I lied. "You know. Give you a thrill."

I felt like a total idiot. But why should I admit that a load of pots on the wall nearly had me scared out of my skin?

"Okay. No more jokes," Stephanie insisted, turning to Seth. "We want to see a real ghost."

"Follow me. I'll show you something that Otto told me about," Seth whispered.

Holding his candle in front of him, he led the way across the kitchen to the wall beside the stove. He lowered his candle in front of a cabinet door. Then he pulled open the cabinet door and moved the candle closer so we could see inside.

"Why are you showing us a kitchen cabinet?" I demanded. "What's scary about that?"

"It's not a cabinet," Seth replied. "It's a dumb waiter. Watch." He reached inside and pulled a rope beside the cabinet shelf. The shelf began to slide up.

He raised the shelf, then lowered it. "See? This dumb waiter is like a tiny lift. It was used to send food from the kitchen to the master bedroom upstairs."

"You mean for midnight snacks?" I joked.

Seth nodded. "The cook would put the food on

the shelf. Then he would pull the rope, and the shelf would carry it upstairs."

"Thrills and chills," I said sarcastically.

"Yeah. Why are you showing it to us?" Stephanie demanded.

Seth brought the candle up close to his face. "Otto told me that this dumb waiter is haunted. A hundred and twenty years ago, things suddenly started to go wrong with it."

Stephanie and I moved closer. I lowered my candle and examined the dumb waiter cabinet. "What went wrong?" I asked.

"Well," Seth began softly, "the cook would put food on the shelf and send it upstairs. But when the shelf reached the bedroom up there, the food was gone."

Stephanie narrowed her eyes at Seth. "It disappeared between the ground and first floor?"

Seth nodded solemnly. His grey eyes glowed in the soft candlelight. "This happened several times. When the shelf reached the first floor, it was empty. The food had vanished."

"Wow," I murmured.

"The cook became very frightened," Seth continued. "He was afraid that the dumb waiter had become haunted. He decided to stop using it. And he ordered everyone on his staff never to use the dumb waiter again."

"And that's the end of the story?" I asked.

Seth shook his head. "And then something horrible happened."

Stephanie's mouth dropped open. "What? What happened?"

"Some kids were visiting the house. One of them was a boy named Jeremy. Jeremy was a real show-off, and very athletic. When he saw the dumb waiter, he decided it would be fun to ride it to the first floor."

"Oh, wow," Stephanie murmured.

I felt a chill. I thought I could guess what was coming.

"So Jeremy squeezed on to the shelf. And one of the other kids pulled the rope. Suddenly the rope caught. The kid couldn't get it to move up or down. Jeremy was stuck somewhere between the floors.

"The other kids called up to him, 'Are you okay?' But Jeremy didn't reply. They started to get very worried. They tugged and tugged, but they couldn't move the rope.

"Then suddenly, the shelf came crashing back down."

"And was Jeremy on it?" I asked eagerly.

Seth shook his head. "There were three covered bowls on the shelf. The kids lifted the lid off the first bowl. Inside was Jeremy's heart, still beating.

"They opened the second bowl. Inside were Jeremy's eyes, still staring in horror. And they opened the third bowl. And saw Jeremy's teeth, still chattering."

The three of us stood silent in the orange glow of candlelight. We stared at the dumb waiter shelf.

I shivered. The pots rattled against the wall. But I was no longer frightened of them. I raised my eyes to Seth. "Do you think that story is true?"

Stephanie laughed. Nervous laughter. "It can't be true," she said.

Seth's face remained solemn. "Do you believe *any* of Otto's stories?" he asked me quietly.

"Well. Yes. No. Some." I couldn't decide.

"Otto swears the story is true," Seth insisted. "But of course, he may just be doing his job. His job is to make this house as scary as possible."

"Otto is a great storyteller," Stephanie murmured. "But enough stories. I want to see a real ghost."

"Follow me," Seth replied. His candle flame dipped low as he spun around.

He led us back through the kitchen, into a long, narrow room at the back. "This is the old butler's pantry," he announced. "All of the food for the house was stored in here."

Stephanie and I stepped past him, raising our candles to see the room better. When I turned around, Seth was closing the pantry door behind us.

Then I saw him turn the lock.

"Hey—what are you doing?" I cried.

"Why are you locking us in here?" Stephanie demanded.

I dropped my candle. It bounced on the hard floor, and the flame went out. The candle rolled under a shelf.

When I glanced back up, Stephanie was storming towards Seth. "Seth—what are you doing?" she demanded angrily. "Unlock that door. This isn't funny!"

I gazed around the long, narrow room. Shelves from floor to ceiling on three walls. No windows. No other door to escape through.

With a sharp cry, Stephanie grabbed for the door handle. But Seth moved quickly to block her way.

"Hey—!" I cried, my heart pounding. I stepped up beside Stephanie. "What's the big idea, Seth?"

His silvery eyes glowed with excitement behind his candle flame. He stared back at us without speaking. The same cold stare I had seen on his face the night before.

Stephanie and I took a step back, huddling close together.

"Sorry, guys. But I played a little trick on you," he said finally.

"Excuse me?" Stephanie cried, more angry than frightened.

"What kind of trick?" I asked.

He pushed back his long, blond hair with his free hand. The flickering candle sent shadows dancing across his face. "My name isn't Seth," he said softly, so softly I could barely hear him.

"But—but—" I stammered.

"My name is Andrew," he said.

Stephanie and I both cried out in surprise.

"But Andrew is the name of the ghost," Stephanie protested. "The ghost who lost his head."

"I am the ghost," he said softly. A dry laugh escaped his lips. More like a cough than a laugh. "I promised you a real ghost tonight. Well . . . here I am."

He blew out the candle. He appeared to vanish with the light.

"But, Seth—" Stephanie started.

"Andrew," he corrected her. "My name is Andrew. My name has been Andrew for more than a hundred years."

"Let us out of here," I pleaded. "We won't tell anyone we saw you. We won't—"

"I can't let you go," he replied in a whisper.

I remembered the story of the sea captain's ghost. When Andrew stumbled into the sea captain's room and saw the old ghost, the sea captain had said the same thing to him. *"Now that you have seen me, I can never let you go."*

"You—you lost your head!" I blurted out.

"So you *can't* be Andrew!" Stephanie cried. "You have a head!"

In the dim light from Stephanie's candle, I could see the sneer spread over Andrew's face. "No," he said softly. "No, no, no. I do not have my head. This is one that I borrowed."

He raised both hands to the side of his face. "Here. Let me show you," he said.

Then he pressed his hands against his cheeks and started to tug the head up from the black turtleneck.

"No! Stop!" Stephanie screeched.

I shut my eyes. I didn't really want to see him pull off his head.

When I opened my eyes, Andrew had lowered his hands.

I gazed once again around the narrow pantry. How could we escape? How could we get out of there? The ghost was blocking the only exit.

"Why did you trick us?" Stephanie asked Andrew. "Why did you bring us here? Why did you lie to us?"

Andrew sighed. "I told you. I borrowed this head." He ran one hand through the hair, then down over the cheek, as if petting it. "I borrowed it. But I have to return it."

Stephanie and I stared back at him in silence, waiting for him to continue. Waiting for him to explain.

"I saw you last night in the tour group," he said finally, his eyes locked on me. "The others couldn't see me. But I made myself visible to you."

"Why?" I asked in a trembling voice.

"Because of your head," he replied. "I liked your head."

"Huh?" A frightened gasp escaped my throat.

He gripped the blond hair again. "I have to return this head, Duane," he said calmly, coldly. "So I'm going to take yours."

A frightened giggle escaped my throat.

Why do people suddenly start laughing when they're terrified? I guess it's because if you don't laugh, you'll scream. Or explode or something.

Trapped in that small, dark room with a hundred-year-old ghost that wanted my head, I felt like laughing, screaming, and exploding all at once!

I stared hard at Andrew, squinting in the dim light. "You're kidding, right?"

He shook his head. His silvery eyes narrowed, hard and cold. "I need your head, Duane," he said softly. He shrugged, as if apologizing. "I'll pull it off quickly. It won't hurt a bit."

"But—but I need it, too!" I sputtered.

"I'm only going to borrow it," Andrew said. He took a step towards us. "I'll return it when I find my own head. Promise."

"You're not cheering me up," I replied.

He took another step towards us.

Stephanie and I backed up a step.

He took a step. We backed up a step.

We didn't have much more room to back up. We were nearly to the back wall of pantry shelves.

Suddenly Stephanie spoke up. "Andrew, we'll find your head!" she offered. Her voice shook.

I turned to her. I'd never seen her scared before. Knowing that Stephanie was scared made me *even more* scared!

"For sure!" I croaked. 'We'll find your real head. We'll search all night. We know this house really well. I'm sure we can find it if you give us a chance."

He stared back at us without replying.

I wanted to get down on my knees and *beg* him to give us a chance.

But I was afraid if I got down on my knees, he'd pull off my head.

"We'll find it, Andrew. I *know* we will," Stephanie insisted.

He shook his head. His borrowed head. "There's no way," he murmured sadly. "How long have I been searching this house? For more than a hundred years. For more than a hundred years, I've searched every hallway, every room, every closet."

He took another step closer. His eyes were locked on my head. I knew he was studying it,

97

thinking about how it would look on his shoulders.

"In all these years, I haven't found my head," Andrew continued. "So what makes you think you can find it tonight?"

'Well . . . uh . . ." Stephanie turned to me.

"Uh . . . maybe we'll get lucky!" I declared.

Lame. How lame can you get?

"Sorry," Andrew murmured. "I need your head, Duane. We're wasting time."

"Give us a chance!" I cried.

He took a step closer. He was studying my hair now. Probably deciding if he should let it grow longer.

"Andrew—please!" I begged.

It was no use. His eyes were glassy now. He reached out both hands and took another step.

Stephanie and I backed up.

"Give me your head, Duane," the ghost whispered.

My back bumped a shelf on the wall behind me.

"I need your head, Duane."

Stephanie and I huddled close and pressed our backs against the shelves.

The ghost floated closer, hands outstretched.

We pressed ourselves tighter against the shelves. My elbow bumped something hard. I heard some heavy objects fall from the shelf.

"I need your head, Duane."

He clenched and unclenched his hands. Two more steps and he'd be close enough to grab me.

"Your head. Give me your head."

I jammed my back against the shelves.

I heard a creaking sound—and the shelf started to slide.

I stumbled back. And realized that the *whole wall* was sliding.

"Wh–what's happening?" I stammered.

The ghost reached for my head. "Gotcha!"

The ghost leaped at me, hands outstretched.

I ducked—and stumbled back as the wall slid away.

The wall made a loud grinding sound as it slowly spun around.

Stephanie fell to the hard floor.

I pulled her up quickly as Andrew made another wild grab for my head.

"A tunnel!" I shouted over the grinding of the wall.

As the wall spun away, it revealed a dark opening. Just big enough to squeeze through.

I pulled Stephanie to the opening—and we squeezed inside.

We found ourselves in a long, low passageway. Some kind of tunnel. Hidden behind the sliding wall.

I'd always heard about old houses that had secret halls and hidden rooms built in them. I never thought I'd be so glad to find one!

Stephanie and I started to run. Our footsteps echoed loudly on the concrete floor.

We ran past bare, concrete walls, cracked and pitted by time. We had to stoop as we ran. The ceiling wasn't as tall as we were!

Stephanie slowed down to glance back. "Is he following us?"

"Just keep running!" I cried. "This tunnel has got to lead out of here! Out of this house! It's *got* to!"

"I can't see *where* it leads!" she replied breathlessly.

The low tunnel stretched out in a straight line. I could see only darkness at the end.

Did it stretch on for ever?

If it did, I'd keep running for ever. I didn't plan to stop running until I was safely outside.

And once I was outside, I planned never to visit Hill House again. And I planned to stay away from ghosts and to keep my head on my shoulders where it belonged.

Big plans.

But plans don't always work out.

"Oh!" Stephanie and I both cried out as we nearly crashed into a solid concrete wall.

The tunnel ended. It just ended.

"It—it doesn't go *anywhere*!" I gasped. Breathing hard, I pounded both fists against the wall. "Who would build a secret tunnel that leads nowhere?"

"Push on the wall," Stephanie cried. "Let's both push. Maybe this wall will slide open, too."

We turned and leaned our shoulders into the wall. And pushed. Groaning and gasping, I pushed with all my strength.

I was still pulling when I heard the scraping footsteps moving towards us down the tunnel.

Andrew!

"Push!" Stephanie cried.

We shoved ourselves against the wall.

"Come on—slide! Slide!" I ordered it.

I glanced back and saw Andrew, jogging slowly, steadily towards us.

"We're trapped," Stephanie moaned. She collapsed against the wall with a sigh.

Andrew came trotting closer.

"Duane—I want your head!" he called, his voice echoing against the concrete walls.

"Trapped," Stephanie murmured.

"Maybe not," I choked out. I pointed into the dark corner. "Look. A ladder."

"Huh?" Stephanie leaped to her feet. She squinted at the ladder. A metal ladder, the rungs blanketed with dust. It led straight up the wall, through a small, square opening in the low ceiling.

To where?

"Give me your head!" the ghost called.

I grabbed the sides of the metal ladder. I

raised a foot on to the first rung and peered straight up.

Into thick blackness. I couldn't see a thing up there.

"Duane—" Stephanie whispered. "We don't know where it leads!"

"It doesn't matter," I replied, starting to climb. "We don't have a choice—do we?"

29

"Where are you going, Duane? I need your head!"

I ignored the ghost's shout and scrambled up the ladder. Stephanie kept bumping me from behind.

My trainers slipped on the thick dust. My hand slid over the cold, metal railings.

"Duane—you can't get away!" Andrew called from down below.

Straight up. Straight up the ladder. Stephanie and I, breathing hard, climbing frantically, as fast as we could climb.

Straight up.

Until the ladder started to tilt.

"Noooo!" I uttered a scream as it spilled forward.

A crumbling, cracking noise drowned out my scream.

It took me a few seconds to realize that the wall was breaking apart. Crumbling into powdery chunks.

And we were falling.

I heard Stephanie scream.

I grabbed the metal railings with both hands—and held on tight.

But the ladder was sailing down now. Tumbling over the cracking, crumbling old wall.

"Ow!" I landed hard. Bounced once. Twice.

My hands flew up and I was tossed off the ladder. I rolled on to my stomach, rolled in the chunks of dirt and concrete of the broken wall.

Stephanie landed on her knees. She shook her head, dazed.

Chunks of wall spilled all around us. Stephanie's hair was covered in dust.

I shielded my eyes and waited for the wall to stop crumbling down.

When I opened my eyes, Andrew stood above me. His hands were balled into fists. His mouth hung open. And he was staring . . . staring *past* me.

I struggled to my feet. Turned to see what he was staring at.

"A hidden room!" Stephanie cried, moving beside me. "A room behind the old wall."

Slipping over the chunks of broken concrete, I took a few steps closer to the room.

And saw what Andrew was staring at.

A head.

A boy's head lying on the floor of the hidden room.

"I don't believe it!" Stephanie gasped. "We found it! We actually found it!"

I swallowed hard. And took a careful step forward.

The head was pale, shimmering white, even in the dim light.

I could see clearly that it was a boy's head. But the long, wavy hair had turned to white. The round eyes glowed green, sparkling like emeralds in the shimmering, pale face.

"The ghost head," I murmured.

I turned back to Andrew. "Your head—we found it for you."

I expected to see a smile on his face. I expected him to shout or jump for joy.

For a hundred years, he had waited for this happy moment. And now his long search was over.

But to my shock, Andrew's face was twisted in horror.

He wasn't even looking at his long lost head. He stared above it. And as he stared, his entire body began to quiver. Frightened cries escaped his lips.

"Andrew—what is your problem?" I demanded.

But I don't think he even heard me.

He stared up at the ceiling, trembling. Hands

balled into tight fists at his sides. Then, slowly, he raised one hand and pointed. "Nooooo," he moaned. "Ohhhh, nooooooo."

I turned to see what had frightened him.

Turned in time to see a filmy figure float down from the ceiling.

At first I thought it was a thin window curtain, falling from above.

But as it curled slowly, softly to the floor, I saw that it had arms. And legs.

I could see right through it!

The air around us suddenly grew cold.

"It—it's a *ghost*!" Stephanie cried, grabbing my arm.

The ghost landed softly, silently on the floor of the hidden room, raising its arms like bird wings.

Stephanie and I both gasped as it raised its arms and stood upright.

It was short and very thin. It wore baggy, old-fashioned-looking trousers and a long-sleeved shirt with a high collar.

A high collar.

A collar.

And no head.

The ghost had no head!

I felt a burst of cold air as it bent down, shimmering, bending, as if made of soft gauze. It reached down. Lifted the head off the floor.

Lifted the head to the stiff, tall collar.

Gently pressed the head into place.

And as the head touched the ghostly, gauzy neck, the green eyes flashed.

The cheeks twitched. The pale white eyebrows arched up and down.

And then the mouth moved.

The ghost turned to us—to Stephanie and me. And the lips moved in a silent "Thank you."

"Thank you."

And then the arms rose into the air. Its green eyes still on us, the ghost floated up into the air. Lighter than air, it floated silently up.

I watched in amazement, my heart pounding, until the ghostly figure vanished in the darkness.

And then Stephanie and I both turned to Andrew at the same time. We had just seen the headless ghost. We had just seen Andrew, the boy from a hundred years ago. We had just watched him collect his head.

But the boy who claimed to be Andrew was still there. He stood behind us, still trembling, his eyes wide, staring into the hidden room, making soft swallowing sounds.

I narrowed my eyes at him. "If you aren't Andrew," I started—"if you aren't the headless ghost—then who *are* you?"

Stephanie turned on the boy, too. "Yeah. Who are you?" she asked angrily.

"If you're not the headless ghost, why did you chase us?" I demanded.

"Well. I . . . uh . . ." The boy raised both hands as if surrendering. Then he started to back away.

He had only gone three or four steps when we heard footsteps coming down the long tunnel.

I turned to Stephanie. Another ghost?

"Who's in here?" a deep voice boomed.

I saw a circle of light from a torch sweeping over the tunnel floor.

"Who is here?" the voice repeated.

I recognized the deep voice. Otto!

"Uh . . . back here," the boy called softly.

"Seth—is that you?" The circle of light floated closer. Otto appeared behind it, squinting at us. "What's going on? What are you doing back here? This part of the house is dangerous. It's all falling apart."

110

"Well . . . we were exploring," Seth started. "And we got lost. It really wasn't our fault."

Otto gazed at Seth sternly. Then his face filled with surprise as his torch washed over Stephanie and me. "You two! How did you get in? What are you doing here?"

"He. . . well. . . he let us in," I answered. I pointed at Seth.

Otto turned back to Seth and shook his head unhappily. "More of your tricks? Were you scaring these kids?"

"Not really, Uncle Otto," Seth replied, keeping his eyes on the ground.

Uncle Otto? So Seth was Otto's nephew!

No wonder he knew so much about Hill House.

"Tell the truth, Seth," Otto insisted. "Were you pretending to be a ghost again? Haven't you played that trick on enough kids? Haven't you scared enough kids to death?"

Seth stood silent.

Otto rubbed his hand back over his smooth, bald head. Then he let out a weary sigh. "We have a business to run here," he told Seth. "Do you want to scare my customers away? Do you want to get the whole neighbourhood upset?"

Seth lowered his head and still didn't reply.

I could see that he was in major trouble. So I decided to jump in. "It's okay, Otto," I said. "He didn't scare us."

"That's right," Stephanie chimed in. "We didn't believe he was a ghost. Did we, Duane?"

"Of course not," I replied. "He didn't fool us for a minute."

"Especially when we saw the *real* ghost," Stephanie added.

Otto turned to her, studying her in the light from the torch. "The *what*?"

"The real ghost!" Stephanie insisted.

"We saw the real ghost, Uncle Otto!" Seth exclaimed. "It was *awesome*!"

Otto rolled his eyes. "Save the jokes, Seth. It's too late at night. You're just trying to get out of trouble."

"No. Really!" I insisted.

"Really!" Seth and Stephanie cried.

"We saw the headless ghost, Uncle Otto. You've got to believe us!" Seth pleaded.

"Sure, sure," Otto murmured. He turned and motioned with his torch. "Come on. Everyone out."

After our scary night at Hill House, Stephanie and I gave up haunting the neighbourhood.

It just wasn't that exciting any more. Especially since we'd seen a real ghost.

We stopped sneaking out at night. We stopped peeking into kids' windows in scary masks. We stopped hiding behind bushes and howling like werewolves in the middle of the night.

We gave up all the scary stuff. And we never even talked about ghosts.

Stephanie and I found other things to be interested in. I tried out for the basketball team at school, and became a forward player.

Stephanie joined the Theatre Arts Club. This spring, she's going to be Dorothy in *The Wizard of Oz*. Either Dorothy or a Munchkin.

We had a good winter. Lots of snow. Lots of unscary fun.

Then late one evening we were heading home

from a birthday party. It was the first warm night of spring. Tulips were blooming in some of the front gardens we passed. The air smelled fresh and sweet.

I stopped in front of Hill House and gazed up at the old mansion. Stephanie stopped beside me. She read my mind. "You want to go in, don't you, Duane?"

I nodded. "How about taking the tour? We haven't been in there since. . ." My voice trailed off.

"Hey, why not?" Stephanie replied.

We climbed the steep hill. Tall weeds brushed the legs of my jeans as I made my way to the front door. The huge old house stood as dark and as creepy as ever.

As Stephanie and I climbed on to the front doorstep, the door creaked open. As it always had.

We stepped into the small front entryway. A few seconds later, Otto bounced into view. Dressed all in black. A friendly smile on his round, bald head.

"You two!" he exclaimed happily. "Welcome back." He called into the front room. "Edna, come and see who is here."

Edna came tottering into the room. "Oh, my!" she cried, pressing a hand against her pale, wrinkled face. "We were wondering if we would see you two again."

114

I gazed into the front room. No other customers.

"Could you take us on the tour?" I asked Otto.

He smiled his toothy smile. "Of course. Wait. I'll get my lantern."

Otto took us around Hill House. He gave us the complete tour.

It was great to see the house again. But it no longer held any secrets for Stephanie and me.

After the tour, we thanked Otto and said good night.

We were halfway down the hill when a police car pulled up to the kerb. A dark-uniformed officer stuck his head out of the passenger window. "What were you kids doing up there?" he called.

Stephanie and I made our way down to the police car. The two officers eyed us suspiciously.

"We just took the tour," I explained, pointing up to Hill House.

"Tour? What tour?" the officer demanded gruffly.

"You know. The haunted house tour," Stephanie replied impatiently.

The police officer stuck his head further out the window. He had blue eyes, and freckles all over his face. "What were you *really* doing up there?" he asked softly.

"We *told* you," I said shrilly. "Taking the tour. That's all."

115

Behind the wheel, the other policeman chuckled. "Maybe a ghost gave them the tour," he told his partner.

"There *are* no tours," the freckle-faced officer said, frowning. "There haven't been any tours in that house for months."

Stephanie and I both uttered cries of surprise.

"The house is empty," the police officers continued. "Shut down. There hasn't been anyone in there all winter. Hill House went out of business three months ago."

"Huh?" Stephanie and I exchanged startled glances. Then we both turned to gaze up at the house.

The grey stone turrets rose up into the purple-black sky. Nothing but darkness all around.

And then I saw a trail of soft light across the front window. Lantern light. Orange and soft as smoke.

In the soft light, I saw Otto and Edna. They floated in front of the window. I could see right through them, as if they were made of gauze.

They're ghosts, too, I realized, staring into the soft, smoky light.

I blinked. And the light faded out.

The Abominable
Snowman of
Pasadena

All my life, I've wanted to see snow.

My name is Jordan Blake. My life has been twelve years of sun, sand and chlorine. I'd never felt cold, *ever*—unless you count air-conditioned supermarkets. And I don't. It doesn't snow in the supermarket.

I'd never felt cold, that is, until the adventure.

Some people think I'm a lucky guy to live in Pasadena, California, where it's always sunny and warm. It's okay, I suppose. But if you've never seen snow, it seems like something out of a science-fiction film.

Fluffy white frozen water that falls out of the sky? It piles up on the ground, and you can make forts and snowmen and snowballs out of it? You have to admit it sounds weird.

One day, my wish came true. I got to see snow at last. And it turned out to be weirder than I thought.

Far weirder.

"Pay attention, kids. This is going to be cool."

Dad's face glowed under the red darkroom light. My sister, Nicole, and I watched him developing film. With a pair of tongs, he dipped a sheet of special paper in a chemical bath.

I've watched Dad develop film all my life. He's a professional photographer. But I'd never seen him so excited about photos before—and that's saying a lot.

Dad takes nature photos. Well, actually, he takes pictures of *everything*!

He never *stops* taking pictures. My mum says that once when I was a baby I saw Dad and screamed. I didn't recognize him without a camera in front of his face. I used to think he had a zoom lens for a nose!

Our house is filled with embarrassing pictures of me—me as a baby in a baggy nappy, me with food all over my face, me crying after scraping my knee, me hitting my sister. . .

Anyway, Dad had just returned from a trip to the Grand Tetons. That's a mountain range in Wyoming—part of the Rocky Mountains. He was all worked up about the pictures he had taken there.

"I wish you kids had seen those bears," Dad said. "A whole family of them. The cubs reminded me of you two—always teasing each other."

Teasing. Ha. Dad thinks Nicole and I *tease*

each other. That's putting it mildly. Nicole—
Miss Know-it-all—drives me crazy.

Sometimes I wish she'd never been born. I've
made it my mission to make *her* feel the same
way. I mean, I try to make her wish she'd never
been born.

"You should have taken us with you to the
Grand Tetons, Dad," I complained.

"It's very cold in Wyoming this time of year,"
Nicole said.

"How do you know, Brainiac?" I jabbed her in
the ribs. "You've never been to Wyoming."

"I read up on it while Dad was away," she
explained. Of course. "There's a picture book
about it in the library if you want to know more,
Jordan. It's just right for you—it's for first
years."

I couldn't think of anything to say back. That's
my problem. I'm too slow with the comebacks.
So I jabbed her again.

"Hey, hey," Dad murmured. "No jabbing. I'm
working here."

Dumb Nicole. Not that she's dumb—she's
really smart. But in a dumb way—that's my
opinion. She's so smart she skipped fifth
grade—and landed in *my* class. She's a year
younger than I am and she's in my class—*and*
she gets straight A's.

Dad's pictures floated in the chemical bath,
slowly becoming clear. "Did it snow in the

mountains while you were there, Dad?" I asked.

"Sure, it snowed," Dad replied. He was concentrating on his work.

"Did you go skiing?" I asked.

Dad shook his head. "I was too busy working."

"How about ice-skating?" Nicole asked.

Nicole acts as if she knows everything. But like me, she'd never seen snow, either. We'd never left Southern California—and you could tell by looking at us.

We're both tanned all year round. Nicole's hair is greenish-blonde from the chlorine in the community pool, and mine is brown with blond streaks. We're in the school swimming team.

"I'll bet it's snowing at Mum's house right now," Nicole said.

"Could be," Dad replied.

Mum and Dad are divorced. Mum has just moved to Pennsylvania. We're going to spend the summer with her. But we stayed in California with Dad to finish the school year.

Mum sent us some pictures of her new house. It was covered with snow. I stared at the pictures, trying to imagine the cold.

"I wish we had stayed at Mum's house while you were gone," I said.

"Jordan, we've been over this." Dad sounded a little impatient. "You can visit your mother when she's settled. She hasn't even bought furniture yet. Where would you sleep?"

"I'd rather sleep on a bare floor than listen to Mrs Witchens snoring on the sofa," I grumbled.

Mrs Witchens stayed with Nicole and me while Dad was away. She was a nightmare. Every morning we had to clean our rooms—she actually inspected them for dust. Every single night she served us liver, Brussels sprouts and fish-head soup with a tall glass of soya milk.

"Her name's not *Witchens*," Nicole corrected me. "It's *Hitchens*."

"I *know* that, *Sicole*," I retorted.

Under the red light in the darkroom, the photos grew clearer. I heard excitement in Dad's voice.

"If these shots come out well, I can publish them in a book," he said. "I will call it *The Brown Bears of Wyoming*, by Garrison Blake. Yes, that has a nice ring to it."

He stopped to pull a photo out of the liquid. It dripped as he stared at it.

"That's weird," he murmured.

"What's weird?" Nicole asked.

He set the picture down without saying anything. Nicole and I glanced at it.

"Dad—" Nicole said. "I hate to break it to you, but that looks like a teddy bear."

It *was* a picture of a teddy bear. A stuffed brown toy bear with a lopsided grin, sitting in the grass. Not the kind of creature you usually find in the Grand Tetons.

"There must be some mistake," Dad said. "Wait until the rest of the photos develop. You'll see. They're amazing."

He pulled up another picture. He studied it. "Huh?"

I grabbed the photo. Another teddy bear.

Dad picked up a third picture. Then a fourth. He moved faster and faster.

"More teddy bears!" he cried. He was frantic. Even in the darkroom, I could see the panic on his face.

"What's going on?" he shouted. "Where are the photos I took?"

"Dad—" Nicole began. "Are you *sure* those bears you saw were real?"

"Of course I'm sure!" Dad boomed at her. "I know the difference between a brown bear and a teddy bear!"

He began to pace back and forth across the darkroom floor. "Did I lose the film somehow?" he murmured, clutching his head with one hand. "Could someone have switched it?"

"The weird part is that you were taking pictures of bears," Nicole noted. "And you ended up with *teddy* bears. That's just so strange."

Dad furiously tapped his hands on the developing table. He muttered to himself. He was starting to lose it.

"Did I lose the film on the plane somehow? Switch hand luggage with someone else, maybe?"

I turned my back to Dad, my shoulders shaking.

"Jordan? What's the matter?" Dad grabbed my shoulders. "Are you all right?"

He spun me around. "Jordan!" Dad cried. "You're—laughing!"

Nicole crossed her arms. She narrowed her eyes at me. "What did you do to Dad's pictures?"

Dad frowned. His voice was calmer now. "All right, Jordan. What's the big joke?"

I gasped for breath, trying to stop laughing. "Don't worry, Dad. Your pictures are okay."

He shoved one of the teddy bear shots in my face. "Okay! You call this okay?!"

"I borrowed your camera before you left for Wyoming," I explained. "I took a bunch of shots of my old teddy bear, for a joke. The rest of the film should have your real bears on it."

I can't resist a good practical joke.

Nicole said, "I had nothing to do with it, Dad. I swear."

Little Miss Goody-Goody.

Dad shook his head. "A joke?" He turned back to the photos and developed a few more. The next shot showed a real bear cub fishing in a stream. Dad laughed.

"You know," he said, putting the picture of the real bear next to one of the teddy bear shots, "they don't look as different as you'd think."

I knew Dad wouldn't stay angry. He never does. That's one reason I like to play tricks on him. He likes to play practical jokes, too.

"Did I ever tell you about the trick I pulled on Joe Morrison?" he asked. Joe Morrison is a photographer friend of Dad's.

"Joe had just got back from Africa, where he had spent months photographing gorillas. He was all excited about these fabulous gorilla shots he'd taken. I saw the pictures, and they were really spectacular.

"Joe had a big meeting set up with the editor of a nature magazine. He was going to go in and show the editor these photos. He was sure the magazine would snap them up in a second.

"Joe didn't know that the editor and I had gone to college together. So I called her up and asked her to help me play a little joke on Joe.

"When Joe went to see her, he showed her the pictures. She looked at them without saying a word.

"Finally he couldn't stand the suspense any longer. He blurted out, 'Well? Do you like them or not?' He's an impatient guy, Joe."

"What did she say?" I asked.

"She frowned and said, 'You're a good photographer, Mr Morrison. But I'm afraid you've been tricked. The creatures you photographed aren't gorillas at all.'"

"Joe's jaw practically fell off his face. He said, 'What do you mean, they're not gorillas?'"

"She said, with a perfectly straight face,

127

'They're people in gorilla suits. Can't you tell the difference between a real gorilla and a man in a gorilla suit, Mr Morrison?'"

I chuckled. Nicole asked, "Then what happened?"

"Joe practically had a nervous breakdown. He snatched up the photos and stared at them. He shouted, 'I don't get it! How could that happen? I spent six months of my life studying people in gorilla suits?'

"Finally the editor burst out laughing and told him it was a joke. She loved the photos and wanted to publish them. Joe wouldn't believe her at first—it took her fifteen minutes to get him to calm down."

Dad and I both laughed.

"I think that's really mean, Dad," Nicole scolded.

I get my joker streak from Dad. Nicole takes after Mum. She's more practical.

"Joe thought it was funny once he'd got over the shock," Dad assured her. "He's played his share of tricks on me, believe me."

Dad swished another photo through the chemical bath. Then he held it up with his tongs. It showed two bear cubs wrestling. He smiled with satisfaction.

"This roll came out great," he said. "But I've got a lot more work to do in here, kids. Go on outside for a while, okay?"

He turned the red light off and flipped on the normal light. Nicole opened the door.

"Don't get all messed up and dirty, though," Dad added. "We're all going out to dinner tonight. I want to celebrate my luck with the brown bears."

"We'll be careful," Nicole promised.

"Speak for yourself," I said.

"I mean it, Jordan," Dad warned.

"Just kidding, Dad."

A wave of heat blasted us when we opened the darkroom door. Nicole and I stepped out into the back garden, blinking in the afternoon sun. It always takes my eyes a long time to adjust after I've been in the darkroom.

"What do you want to do?" Nicole asked.

"I don't know," I replied. "It's so hot. It's too hot to do much of anything."

Nicole closed her eyes and zoned out for a minute.

"Nicole?" I nudged her. "Nicole? What are you doing?"

"I'm thinking about the snow in Dad's pictures of the Grand Tetons. I thought it would make me feel cooler."

She stood perfectly still with her eyes closed. A bead of sweat dripped down her forehead.

"Well?" I asked. "Is it working?"

She opened her eyes and shook her head. "No. How can I imagine snow if I've never felt it?"

"Good point." I sighed and gazed around me.

We live in a subdivision in the suburbs of Pasadena. There are only three different kinds of houses in our neighbourhood. The same three house styles are repeated for miles around.

It's so boring to look at, it makes me feel even hotter, somehow. Each block has a couple of palm trees, not enough to give much shade. There's a vacant lot across the street from us, next door to the Millers'. The most exciting feature of our back garden—maybe the whole block—is Dad's disgusting compost heap.

I squinted and stared some more. Everything appeared bleached in the sunlight. Even the grass looked almost white.

"I'm so bored I could scream," I complained.

"Let's ride our bikes," Nicole suggested. "Maybe the breeze will cool us off."

"Maybe Lauren will want to go with us," I added.

Lauren Sax lives next door to us. She's in our class at school. I see her so often, she might as well be my sister.

We rolled out our bikes from the garage and walked them over to Lauren's. We left our bikes at the side of her house. Then we went round the back.

We found Lauren sitting on a towel under a palm tree in her back garden. Nicole sat beside Lauren on the towel. I leaned against the tree.

"It's so hot!" Lauren whined. She tugged on her yellow shorts. She's tall and muscular, with long brown hair and a fringe.

She has a nasal voice, good for complaining. "This is supposed to be winter. It's winter everywhere else. A normal winter has snow and ice and sleet and freezing rain and cold, cold air. What do we get? Nothing but sun! Why do we have to be so *hot*?"

Suddenly I felt a pain in my back.

"Ow!" I jerked forward. Something stabbed me. Something stinging sharp—and ice cold! My face twisted in pain.

"Jordan!" Nicole gasped. "What's wrong? What's wrong?"

I clutched the icy spot on my back. "What is it?" I cried. "It's so cold!"

Nicole jumped to her feet and examined my back. "Jordan, you've been stabbed!" she announced. "With a purple Popsicle!"

As I turned around I heard mean laughter. The Miller twins jumped out from behind the tree.

I should've known. The Miller twins—Kyle and Kara. The twin pug noses, the beady little eyes, the matching short-cropped red hair. Yuck. They carried twin Super Soakers, red ones.

The Miller twins love practical jokes. They're worse than I am. And much meaner.

Everyone in the neighbourhood is afraid of them. They pounce on little kids waiting at the bus stop and rob them of their lunch money. Once they blew up the Saxes' letterbox with a stink bomb. Last year, Kyle winded me during a basketball game. He thought it was fun to watch me turn purple.

The Millers like to pick on me more than anyone, for some reason.

Kara is just as scary as her brother Kyle. I hate to admit it, but Kara can take me out with one punch. I know that for a fact. She gave me a black eye last summer.

"'Oh, it's so hot. It's so hot!'" Kara sneered, making fun of Lauren's whiny voice.

Kyle flipped his Super Soaker from one hand to the other behind his back. He tried to make it look like a really complicated move.

"Arnold taught me how to do that," he bragged.

Kyle wanted me to think he was talking about Arnold Schwarzenegger. He claims he knows Arnold. I have my doubts.

Nicole tugged on the back of my shirt. "Dad's going to kill you, Jordan," she said.

"Why?"

I craned my neck backwards. The back of my white polo shirt was stained dark purple.

"Oh, great," I muttered.

"Dad said not to get messed up," Nicole reminded me. As if I needed to be reminded.

"Don't worry, Jordan," Kyle said. "We'll clean it off for you."

"Uh—that's okay," I murmured, backing away. Whatever Kyle meant by "clean it off", I knew I wouldn't like it.

I was right.

He and Kara raised their Super Soakers and squirted me, Nicole and Lauren.

"Stop it!" Lauren screamed. "You're getting us all wet!"

Kyle and Kara laughed their maniac laughs. "You *said* you were hot!"

They drenched us. My shirt was so wet I could wring a glass of water out of it. I glared at them.

Kyle shrugged. "We were only trying to help."

Yeah. Sure they were.

I should've been grateful that all they did was soak us. We got off easily.

I can't stand the Miller twins. Neither can Nicole and Lauren. They think they're so hot. Just because they're thirteen and they have a swimming pool in their back garden.

Their father works at a film studio. They're always bragging about how they go to sneak previews and hang out with film stars.

I haven't seen a film star show up at their house yet. Not once.

"Aw, you're all wet," Kara said, sneering. "Why don't you take a bike ride to dry off?"

Nicole and I exchanged glances. When we're alone, we don't get along so well. But when the Millers are around, we have to stick together.

We knew the Millers too well. They wouldn't mention our bikes without a reason. A bad reason.

"What did you do to our bikes?" Nicole demanded.

The Millers faked wide-eyed innocence. "Who—us? We didn't do anything to your precious bikes. Go and see for yourself."

Nicole and I glanced around the side of Lauren's house, where we'd left our bikes.

"They look okay from here," Nicole whispered.

"There's something wrong with them," I said. "They look weird."

We approached our bikes. They looked weird all right. The handlebars had been unscrewed and twisted backwards.

"Hope you have reverse gear," Kyle sniggered.

Normally, I'm not the kind of guy who goes around getting into fights. But something in me snapped. This time Kyle and Kara had gone too far.

I jumped on Kyle. We tumbled to the ground. We wrestled. I tried to pin him with my knee, but he pushed me over on to my side.

"Stop it!" Nicole screamed. "Stop it!"

Kyle rolled me on to my back. "You thought you could jump me, Jordan? You're too big a wimp!"

I kicked him. He pinned my shoulder to the ground with one knee.

Nicole shouted hysterically, "Jordan! Look out!"

I glanced up. Kara stood over me, clutching a

rock the size of her head. A mean grin spread across her face.

"Drop it, Kara!" Kyle ordered.

I tried to roll out of the way, but I couldn't move. Kyle had me pinned.

Kara heaved the rock. Then she let it drop— right on to my head.

I squeezed my eyes shut.

The rock landed on my forehead—and bounced off.

I opened my eyes. Kara laughed like a hyena. She picked up the rock and dropped it on my face again. It bounced off, just like the first time.

Lauren grabbed it. "It's made of sponge," she announced. She squeezed it in her hand. "It's a fake."

Kyle laughed. "It's a film prop, moron."

"You should've seen your face," Kara added. "What a chicken!"

I kicked Kyle off me and pounced on him again. This time I was so mad I had the strength of two Kyles. I wrestled him to the ground. I had him pinned!

"What's going on, guys?"

Uh-oh. Dad.

I leaped to my feet. "Hi, Dad. We were just mucking around."

Kyle sat up, rubbing his elbow.

Dad didn't even seem to notice that we'd been fighting. He was excited about something.

"Listen, kids—I have great news. *Wilderness* magazine just called. They want to fly me to Alaska!"

"Great, Dad," I said sarcastically. "You get to go on another exciting trip while we stay here and die of boredom."

"And heat," Nicole added.

Dad laughed. "I called Mrs Hitchens to see if she could come and stay with you again—" he began.

"Not Mrs Hitchens again!" I cried. "Dad, she's horrible! I can't stand her cooking. I'll starve to death if she stays with us!"

"You will not, Jordan," Nicole said. "Even if you ate only bread and water, you could survive a week easily."

"Nicole? Jordan? Hello?" Dad said, knocking lightly on our heads. "Will you please listen to me? I haven't finished yet."

"Sorry, Dad."

"Anyway, Mrs Hitchens can't come. So, I guess you two will just have to come along with me."

"To Alaska?" I cried. I was too excited to believe it.

"Hurray!" Nicole yelled. We jumped up and down.

"You guys are so lucky!" Lauren said. Kara and Kyle stood by. Saying nothing.

"We're going to Alaska!" I shouted. "We'll get to see snow! Tons of snow! Alaskan snow!"

I was thrilled. And Dad hadn't even told us the interesting part yet.

"It's a strange project," Dad continued. "They want me to track down some kind of snow creature—an Abominable Snowman."

"Wow!" I gasped.

Kyle and Kara snorted.

Nicole shook her head. "An Abominable Snowman? Has anybody really seen him?"

Dad nodded. "Some kind of snow creature has been spotted. Who knows what it really is? Whatever it is, the magazine wants me to shoot photos of it. I'm sure it's a wild-goose chase. There's no such thing as an Abominable Snowman."

"So why are you going?" Nicole asked.

I poked her in the ribs. "Who cares? We're going to Alaska!"

"The magazine is paying a big fee," Dad explained. "And even if we don't find a snow creature, I'll still get some great shots of the tundra."

Lauren asked, "What's a tundra?"

Dad began to reply, but Nicole stepped forward. "I'll handle this one, Dad," she interrupted. I felt like screaming. She does that in school all the time, too.

"A tundra is a huge frozen plain. It exists in the Arctic, in Alaska, and in Russia. The word *tundra* comes from the Russian, meaning—"

I clapped my hand over her big mouth. "Any other questions, Lauren?"

Lauren shook her head. "That's all I needed to know."

"Egghead here goes on for ever if you don't stop her." I let go of Nicole's mouth. She stuck her tongue out at me.

"This trip is going to be great," I cried happily. "We'll see ice and snow for real! We're going hunting for an Abominable Snowman! Awesome!"

An hour earlier we'd been bored out of our minds. Now suddenly everything had changed.

Dad smiled. "I've got to go back to the darkroom for a while. Don't forget—we're going out to dinner tonight." He wandered back across the lawn and into the house.

As soon as Dad was gone, Kara started laughing. "An Abominable Snowman! What a joke!"

Typical Kara—she was too chicken to say a word while Dad was around.

Kyle made fun of me, jumping up and down and squealing, "Alaska! Alaska! I'll get to see snow!"

"You will both probably turn blue and freeze," Kara sneered.

"*We'll* be fine," Nicole said. "It's *your* turn to freeze!" She grabbed Kara's Super Soaker and sent a spray of water into Kara's face.

"Stop it!" Kyle shouted. He dived at Nicole. Nicole laughed and ran away, turning around to soak them every few feet.

"Give that back!" Kara yelled.

The Millers chased Nicole. Kyle raised his Super Soaker and let Nicole have it in the back.

Lauren and I ran after them. Nicole raced into our back garden. She turned around and squirted the Millers again.

"You can't catch me!" she cried, shooting and walking backwards.

She was backing right into Dad's compost heap.

Should I warn her? I thought.

No way.

"Take that!" she shouted, blasting the Millers with water.

Then she slipped and fell backwards—into the compost heap.

"Yuck," Lauren groaned.

Nicole stood up slowly. Greenish-brown slime oozed in her hair and dripped down her back, her arms, and her legs. "Ugh!" she screamed, frantically wiping the mess off her hands. "Uggghhh!"

141

We all stood and stared. She looked like some kind of Abominable Snowman herself. All covered in goo.

We were still staring when Dad popped his head out the back door. "You kids ready to go to dinner?" he called.

"There it is!" Dad shouted over the roar of the small plane's engine. "Iknek. That's the airstrip."

I stared out the window at the tiny brown patch where we'd be landing. For the last half hour I'd seen nothing but miles and miles of snow. Wow. It was so *white*!

It was cool the way the snow sparkled in the sunlight. It made me think of Christmas carols. I couldn't get "Winter Wonderland" out of my head—and it was driving me crazy!

I watched for giant footprints as we flew. How big would an Abominable Snowman's footsteps be? Big enough to see from a low-flying plane?

"I hope there's a restaurant down there," Nicole said. "I'm starving."

Dad patted her shoulder. "We'll have a big, hot meal before we set out. But after that, it's camping food."

"How are we going to build a fire in the snow?" Nicole asked.

"We'll be staying in a little cabin," Dad replied. "It's a long way out in the tundra, but it's better than sleeping in tents. There should be a stove in the cabin. I *hope* so, anyway."

"Can we build an igloo and sleep in that?" I asked. "Or dig an ice cave?"

"You can't build an igloo just like that, Jordan," Nicole snapped. "It's not like a snow fort or something. Right, Dad?"

Dad took the lens cap off his camera and started taking pictures through the plane window. "Sure," he said absently. "Uh-huh."

Nicole turned to the window, too. I mimicked her behind her back. *You can't build an igloo just like that*, I mouthed. She acts like she's my teacher or something. It's really embarrassing when she does it in front of everybody at school.

"How are we going to find the cabin?" Nicole asked. "Everything looks the same in all this snow."

Dad turned and snapped a picture of her. "Did you say something, Nicole?"

"I was wondering how we're going to find the cabin," Nicole repeated. "Do you know how to use a compass, Dad?"

"A compass? No, but that doesn't matter. A man named Arthur Maxwell is supposed to meet us at the airport. He'll be our guide through the tundra."

"I know Arthur," the pilot shouted back to

us. "He's an old musher from way back. Knows everything about dogs and sledges. He knows this part of Alaska better than anybody, I bet."

"Maybe he's seen the Abominable Snowman," I suggested.

"How do you know there is such a thing?" Nicole taunted. "We haven't seen any sign of him yet."

"Nicole, people have *seen* him with their own eyes," I replied. "And if there's no such thing, what are we doing here?"

"Some people *say* they've seen him," Nicole said. "Or maybe they *think* they've seen one. I won't believe it until I get more facts."

The plane circled the small town. I played with the zipper on my new Arctic jacket. I'd been hungry a few minutes earlier, but now I was too excited to think about food.

There really is an Abominable Snowman down there, I thought. I know there is. I felt a chill, despite a blast of hot air from the plane's heater.

What if we find him? What will happen then?

What will happen if the Abominable Snowman doesn't like to be photographed?

The plane flew very low now, getting ready to land. We touched down with a bump and taxied along the runway. The plane lurched as the pilot put on the brakes.

Something big loomed at the end of the run-way. Something huge, white and monstrous.

"Dad, look!" I cried. "I see him! The Abominable Snowman!"

The plane squealed to a stop right in front of the big monster.

Dad, Nicole and the pilot all laughed—at *me*.

I hate that. But I couldn't blame them. The big white monster was a polar bear.

A statue of a polar bear.

"The polar bear is the symbol of the town," the pilot explained.

"Oh," I murmured. I knew I was blushing. I turned away.

"Jordan knew that," Dad said. "He was just playing one of his practical jokes."

"Uh—yeah." I went along with it. "I knew it was a statue all along."

"You did not, Jordan," Nicole said. "You were really scared!"

I punched Nicole in the arm. "I was not! It was a joke."

Dad put an arm around each of us. "Isn't it

147

great the way these two play with each other?" he said to the pilot.

"If you say so," the pilot replied.

We hopped out of the plane. The pilot opened the cargo hold. Nicole and I grabbed our rucksacks.

Dad had brought a huge, airtight trunk for film, cameras, food, sleeping bags and other supplies. The pilot helped him carry it off the airstrip.

The trunk was so big, Dad could fit inside it. It reminded me of a red plastic coffin.

Iknek Airport was like a tiny wooden house, just two rooms. Two pilots in leather jackets sat at a table playing cards.

A tall, brawny man with dark hair, a thick beard and leathery skin stood up and crossed the room to greet us. His grey parka hung open over a flannel shirt and deerskin trousers.

This must be our guide, I realized.

"Mr Blake?" the man said to Dad. His voice was low and hoarse. "I'm Arthur Maxwell. Need some help there?" He grabbed one end of the trunk from the pilot.

"This is an awfully big trunk you brought," Arthur added. "Do you really need all this stuff?"

Dad reddened. "I've got a lot of cameras, tripods and things... Well, maybe I over-packed."

Arthur frowned at me and Nicole. "I'd say so."

"Call me Garry," Dad said. "These are my kids, Jordan and Nicole." He nodded towards us.

Nicole said "Hi," and I added, "Nice to meet you." I can be polite when I have to be.

Arthur stared at us. Then he grunted.

"You didn't mention kids," he mumbled to Dad after a minute.

"I'm sure I did," Dad protested.

"I don't remember it," Arthur replied, frowning.

Everyone was silent. We pushed through the airport door and started down the muddy road.

"I'm hungry," I said. "Let's go into town and get some food."

"How far is it to town, Arthur?" Dad asked.

"How far?" Arthur echoed. "You're looking at it."

I stared around in surprise. There was only one road. It began at the airport and ended in a pile of snow about two blocks away. A few wooden buildings were sprinkled along it.

"This is it?" I cried.

"It's not Pasadena," Arthur grumbled. "But we call it home."

He led us down the muddy road to a café called Betty's.

"I guess you're hungry," he grumbled. "Might as well eat a hot meal before we set out."

We settled into a booth by a window. Nicole and I ordered hamburgers, french fries and Cokes. Dad and Arthur ordered coffee and beef stew.

"I've got a sledge and four dogs ready to go," Arthur announced. "The dogs can pull this trunk of yours and the other supplies. We'll walk beside the sledge."

"That sounds fine," Dad said.

"Whoa!" I protested. "We're *walking*? How far?"

"Ten miles or so," Arthur replied.

"Ten miles!" I'd never walked that far before. "Why do we have to walk? Why can't we take a helicopter or something?"

"Because I want to take photos along the way, Jordan," Dad explained. "The landscape is fascinating. You never know what we'll come across."

Maybe we'll come across the Abominable Snowman, I thought. That would be cool.

Our food arrived. We all ate in silence. Arthur wouldn't look me in the eye. He wouldn't look any of us in the eye. He stared out of the window while he ate. Outside on the street, a Jeep drove by.

"Have you ever seen this snow creature we're looking for?" Dad asked Arthur.

Arthur speared a piece of meat with his fork and popped it into his mouth. He chewed. He chewed some more. Dad, Nicole and I all watched him, waiting for his answer.

Finally he swallowed. "Never seen it," he said. "Heard about it, though. Lots of stories."

I waited to hear one of the stories. But Arthur kept on eating.

I couldn't stand waiting any longer. "What kind of stories?"

He swabbed at some gravy with his bread. He stuffed it into his mouth. Chewed. Swallowed.

"A couple of people in town," he said. "They've seen the monster."

"Where?" Dad asked.

"Out by the big snow ridge," Arthur said. "Beyond the musher's cabin. Where we're staying."

"What does he look like?" I asked.

"They say he's big," Arthur said. "Big and covered with brown fur. You might think he's a bear. But he's not. He walks on two feet like a man."

I shuddered. The Abominable Snowman sounded a lot like a vicious cave monster I'd seen in a horror film once.

Arthur shook his head. "Personally, I hope we never find him."

Dad's jaw dropped. "But that's what we're here for. It's my job to find him—if he exists."

"He exists all right," Arthur declared. "Friend of mine—another musher—he was out in a blizzard one day. Ran smack into the snow monster."

"What happened?" I asked.

"You don't want to know." Arthur stuffed more bread into his mouth.

"We certainly do want to know," Dad persisted.

Arthur stroked his beard. "The monster picked up one of the dogs and made off with him. My friend chased after him, trying to get the dog back. Never found him. But he could hear the dog whining. Pitiful howls. Whatever happened to that dog—it sounded pretty bad."

"He's probably a carnivore," Nicole said. "A meat-eater. Most animals around here are. There's so little vegetation—"

I jabbed Nicole. "I want to hear about the snowman—not your stupid nature facts."

Arthur flashed Nicole an annoyed glance. I figured he was thinking, What planet is *she* from? That's what I'm usually thinking, anyway.

He cleared his throat and continued. "My friend came back to town. He and another guy went out to try and capture the snow monster. Darn foolish, if you ask me."

"What happened to them?" I asked.

"Don't know," Arthur said. "They never came back."

"Huh?" I gaped at the big guide. I swallowed hard. "Excuse me? Did you say they never came back?"

Arthur nodded solemnly. "They never came back."

"Maybe they got lost in the tundra," Dad suggested.

"Doubt it," Arthur said. "Those two knew what they were doing. The monster killed them. That's what happened."

He paused to butter another slice of bread.

"Close your mouth, Jordan," Nicole said. "I don't want to look at your chewed-up french fries."

I suppose my mouth had been hanging open. I shut it and swallowed.

Arthur is such a weird guy, I thought. But he's not lying to us. He definitely believes in the Abominable Snowman.

Nicole asked him, "Has anyone else seen the snow monster?"

"Yep. A couple of TV people from New York. They heard about what happened to my friend and came to town to investigate. They set out into the tundra. Never came back, either. We

154

found one of them frozen to death in a block of ice. Who knows what became of the other?

"Then Mrs Carter—she lives at the end of Main Street—she saw the snow monster a few days later," Arthur continued in a low voice. "She was looking through her telescope and spied him out in the tundra. He was chewing on bones, she said. Don't believe me, go and ask her yourself."

Dad made a noise. I glanced at him. He was trying to keep from laughing.

I didn't see what was so funny. This snow monster sounded pretty scary to me.

Arthur glared at Dad. "You don't have to believe me if you don't want to, Mr Blake," he said.

"Call me Garry," Dad repeated.

"I'll call you what I please, Mr Blake," Arthur said sharply. "What I'm telling you is true. That monster is real—and he's a killer! You're taking a big risk, chasing after him. No one has ever caught him. Anyone who goes out after him . . . doesn't return."

"We'll take our chances," Dad said. "I've heard stories like this before, in other parts of the world. Stories about monsters in the jungle or weird creatures in the ocean. So far the stories have never turned out to be true. I have a feeling the Abominable Snowman will be no different."

Part of me really wanted to see the snow

creature. But part of me hoped Dad was right. I don't deserve to die, I thought—just because I want to see snow!

"Well," Dad said, wiping his mouth. "Let's get going. Everybody ready?"

"I'm ready," Nicole piped up.

"Me too," I said. I couldn't wait to get out in the snow.

Arthur said nothing. Dad paid the lunch bill.

We waited for change. "Dad," I asked, "what if the Abominable Snowman is real? What if we run into him? What will we do?"

He pulled something small and black out of his coat pocket.

"This is a radio transmitter," he explained. "If we get into any kind of trouble out in the wilderness, I can radio the ranger station in town. They'll send a helicopter to rescue us."

"What kind of trouble, Dad?" Nicole asked.

"I'm sure there won't be any trouble," Dad assured us. "But it's good to be prepared for emergencies. Right, Arthur?"

Arthur smacked his lips and cleared his throat. But he didn't reply. I figured he was angry because Dad didn't believe his stories about the snow monster.

Dad returned the radio transmitter to his coat pocket. He left a tip for the waitress. Then we spilled outside into the cold Alaskan air, ready to head out for the frozen tundra.

Was an Abominable Snowman waiting for us somewhere out there?

We would soon find out.

Smack!

Bull's-eye. I hit Nicole in the middle of her rucksack with a snowball.

"Dad!" Nicole cried. "Jordan hit me with a snowball!"

Dad had his camera in front of his face, clicking away, as usual. "Good for you, Nicole," he said absently. Nicole rolled her eyes.

Then she ripped off my ski cap. She stuffed it with snow and smushed it on top of my head.

Snow trickled down my face. The cold burned my skin.

At first I thought snow was cool. I could mush it up in my hand to make snowballs. Fall down in it without getting hurt. Put it on my tongue and let it melt into water.

But I was beginning to feel the cold. My toes and fingers were getting numb. We had already walked two miles out of town. When I looked back, I couldn't see it. I could see only snow and sky.

Only eight more miles to the cabin, I thought, wiggling my fingers inside my gloves. Eight more miles! It was going to take for ever. And all around us, nothing but snow—miles and miles of it.

Dad and Arthur trudged beside the dog-sled. Arthur had brought along four Alaskan huskies—Binko, Rocky, Tin-tin and Nicole's favourite, Lars. They pulled Dad's big trunk and the other supplies in a long, narrow sledge.

Nicole and I each carried a rucksack filled with emergency food and other supplies. Just in case, Dad said.

In case of what? I wondered. In case we get lost? In case the dogs run away with the sledge? In case the Abominable Snowman captures us?

Dad snapped pictures of the dogs, of us, of Arthur, of the snow.

Nicole threw herself backwards into a snow-drift. "Look—an angel!" she cried, waving her arms up and down.

She jumped up and we checked out the snow angel. "Cool," I admitted. I lay on my back to make one, too. When Nicole came closer to inspect it, I whopped her with a snowball.

"Hey!" she cried. "I'm going to get you for that!"

I leaped up and darted away. The deep snow crunched under my shoes.

Nicole ran after me. We raced ahead of the dog-sled.

"Be careful, kids!" Dad called after us. "Stay out of trouble!"

I stumbled in the snow. Nicole pounced on me. I wriggled free and bolted away.

What kind of trouble could we get into? I thought as my feet crunched along. There's nothing but snow for miles around. We couldn't even get *lost* out here!

I turned around and ran backwards, waving at Nicole. "Try and catch me, Miss Factoid!" I teased.

"Name-calling is so immature!" she yelled, chasing after me.

Then she stopped and pointed behind me. "Jordan! Look out!"

"Hey—I'm not falling for that old trick," I called back. I skipped backwards through the snow. I didn't want to take my eyes off her, in case she planned to pelt me with snowballs.

"Jordan, I mean it!" she screamed. "Stop!"

Thud!

I landed hard on my back in a pile of snow. "Uh!" I grunted, stunned.

I struggled to catch my breath. Then I stared around me.

I had fallen down some kind of deep crevasse. I sat shivering in the pile of snow, surrounded by narrow cliffs of bluish ice and rock.

I stood and looked up. The opening of the crevasse was at least twenty feet above me. Frantically, I clutched at the icy walls. I grabbed on to a jutting rock and fumbled for a foothold, hoping to climb out.

I hoisted myself up a couple of feet. Then my hand slipped and I slid back to the bottom. I tried again. The ice was too slick.

How would I ever get out of here?

Where were Dad and Nicole? I tried to warm my cheeks with my gloves. Why don't they come to get me? I'm going to freeze down here!

Nicole's face appeared at the top of the crevasse. I'd never been so happy to see her in my life.

"Jordan? Are you all right?"

"Get me out of here!" I shouted.

"Don't worry," Nicole assured me. "Dad's coming."

I leaned against the pit wall. The sunlight didn't reach the bottom. My toes felt ready to break off. They were so cold! I jumped up and down to keep warm.

A few minutes later, I heard Dad's voice. "Jordan? Are you hurt?"

"No, Dad!" I called up to him. He, Nicole and Arthur all stared down at me from above.

"Arthur is going to lower a rope down to you," Dad instructed. "Hold on to it, and we'll hoist you out of there."

I stepped aside as Arthur tossed one end of a knotted rope into the crevasse. I clutched the rope with my gloved hands.

Arthur shouted, "Heave!"

Dad and Arthur tugged on the rope. I planted my feet in footholds in the ice, bracing myself against the side of the crevasse. The rope slipped out of my hands. I clutched it tighter.

"Hold on, Jordan!" Dad called.

They pulled again. My arms felt as if they were going to be yanked out of their sockets. "Ow!" I cried. "Careful!"

Slowly they hoisted me to the top of the crevasse. I wasn't much help—my feet kept slipping on the icy walls. Dad and Arthur each took one of my hands and dragged me out of the pit.

I lay on the snow, trying to catch my breath.

Dad tested my arms and legs for sprains and breaks. "You sure you're all right?" he asked.

I nodded.

"It was a mistake to haul kids along," Arthur grumbled. "The snow is not as solid as it looks, you know. If we hadn't seen you fall, we never would have found you."

"We've got to be more careful," Dad agreed. "I want you both to stick close to the sled." He leaned over the side of the crevasse and snapped a picture.

I stood up and brushed the snow from the seat of my trousers. "I'll be careful from now on," I promised.

"Good," Dad said.

"We'd better push on," Arthur said.

We started walking again across the snow. I gave Nicole a shove once in a while, and she shoved me back. But we were quieter now. Neither of us wanted to end up frozen to death at the bottom of a snow hole.

Dad snapped away as we walked. "How much further to the cabin?" he asked Arthur.

"Another couple of miles," Arthur replied. He

pointed to a steep mountain of snow in the distance. "See that snow rise, about ten miles off? That's where the monster was last spotted."

The Abominable Snowman had been seen by that snow rise, I thought. Where was he now?

Could he see us coming? Was he hiding somewhere, watching us?

I kept my eyes on the snow rise as we walked. It seemed to grow bigger as we came closer to it. The snow rise was dotted with pine trees and boulders.

After about an hour, a tiny brown speck appeared a mile or so away.

"That's the abandoned musher's cabin where we'll stop for the night," Dad explained. He rubbed his gloves together and added, "It certainly will be nice to sit by a roaring fire."

I clapped my gloves together to keep the blood flowing through my hands. "I can't wait," I agreed. "It must be minus two thousand degrees out here!"

"Actually, it's about minus ten," Nicole stated. "At least, that's the average temperature for this area at this time of year."

"Thank you, Weather Girl," I joked. "And now for sports. Arthur?"

Arthur frowned into his beard. I guess he didn't get the joke.

He fell behind us a little to check the back of

the sled. Dad turned around to snap Arthur's picture.

"When we get to the musher's cabin I'll take a few more scenery photos," Dad said, as he changed his film. "Maybe I'll photograph the cabin, too. Then we'll all turn in. We have a big day tomorrow."

By the time we reached the cabin it was almost eight o'clock at night.

"Took us too long to get here," Arthur grumbled. "We left town after lunch. It should've taken us about five hours. The kids having *accidents* and all is slowing us down."

Dad stood a few feet away from him, taking a portrait photo of Arthur while he talked.

"Mr Blake, did you hear me?" Arthur growled. "Stop taking my picture!"

"What?" Dad said, letting his camera drop to his chest. "Oh, yeah—the kids. Bet they're hungry."

I explored the musher's cabin. It didn't take long. The tiny wooden shack was empty except for an old wood-burning stove and a couple of shabby bunks.

"Why is the cabin so empty?" Nicole asked.

"Mushers don't stop here any more," Arthur explained. "They're afraid of the monster."

I didn't like the sound of that. I glanced at Nicole. She rolled her eyes.

Arthur bedded the dogs in a lean-to outside

165

the cabin. The lean-to was a shed built against the back cabin wall. It was filled with straw for the dogs to sleep on. I spotted a rusty old dog-sled propped in a corner.

Then Arthur lit a fire and began to fix some supper.

"Tomorrow we'll search for this so-called monster," Dad announced. "Everybody get a good night's sleep."

After supper we crawled into our sleeping bags. I lay awake for a long time, listening to the howling wind outside. Listening for the thudding footsteps of an Abominable Snowman.

"Nicole, get off me!" She rolled over in her sleeping bag and jabbed her elbow into my ribs. I knocked her arm away and snuggled deeper inside my own toasty warm sleeping bag.

Nicole opened her eyes. Bright morning sunshine streamed into the cabin.

"I'll be back in a minute to fix breakfast, kids," Dad said. He sat in a chair, lacing up his snow boots. "First I'm going out to check on the dogs. Arthur went out to feed them a few minutes ago."

He bundled up and stepped outside. I rubbed my nose—it was cold. The fire in the stove had gone out during the night. No one had relit it yet.

I forced myself to climb out of my sleeping

bag and start pulling on clothes. Nicole began dressing, too.

"Do you think there's a hot shower in this dump?" I wondered aloud.

Nicole smirked at me. "You know perfectly well there's no hot shower, Jordan!"

"Oh, wow! This is incredible!" I heard Dad's shout from outside.

I jammed my feet into my boots and raced out of the door. Nicole pushed right behind me.

Dad stood at the side of the musher's cabin, pointing in shock at the ground.

I gazed down—and saw deep footprints in the snow. Huge footprints. *Enormous* footprints.

So big that only a monster could have made them.

"Unbelievable," Dad murmured, staring at the snow.

Arthur hurried over from the lean-to. He stopped when he saw the prints.

"No!" he cried. "He was here!"

His ruddy face grew pale. His jaw trembled with terror.

"We've got to get away from here—now!" he said to Dad in a low, frightened voice.

Dad tried to calm him down. "Hold on a minute. Let's not jump to conclusions."

"We're in terrible danger!" Arthur insisted. "The monster is nearby! He'll rip us all to shreds!"

Nicole knelt in the snow, studying the footprints. "Do you think they're real?" she asked. "Real Abominable Snowman footprints?"

She thinks they're real, I thought. She believes.

168

Dad knelt beside her. "They look pretty real to me."

Then I saw a light glimmer in his eyes. He lifted his head and squinted at me suspiciously.

I backed away.

"Jordan!" Nicole cried in an accusing voice.

I couldn't help it. I started laughing.

Dad shook his head. "Jordan. I should've known."

"What?" Arthur looked confused—and then angry. "You mean the kid made these prints? It's a joke?"

"I'm afraid so, Arthur," Dad sighed.

Arthur scowled at me. Beneath his beard, his face reddened to the colour of a slab of raw steak.

I cowered. I couldn't help it. Arthur scared me. He really didn't like kids—especially not kids who play jokes.

"I've got work to do," Arthur muttered. He turned and stomped away through the snow.

"Jordan, you idiot," Nicole said. "When did you do it?"

"I woke up early this morning and sneaked out," I admitted. "You were all sleeping. I carved the footprints over my own prints, with my gloves. Then I stepped in the prints on my way back, to cover my tracks.

"You believed," I added, jabbing a finger at Nicole. "For a minute there, you believed in the snow monster."

"I did not!" Nicole protested.

"Yes, you did. I got you to believe!"

I glanced from Nicole's peevish face to Dad's stern one. "Don't you think it's funny?" I asked. "It's just a joke!"

Usually Dad liked my jokes.

Not this time.

"Jordan, we're not at home in Pasadena now. We're out in the middle of nowhere. The wilds of Alaska. Things could get very dangerous. You saw that yesterday when you fell down the crevasse."

I nodded and hung my head.

"I'm serious, Jordan," Dad warned me. "No more practical jokes. I'm here to work. And I don't want anything to happen to you, or Nicole, or any of us. Understood?"

"Yes, Dad."

No one said anything for a minute. Then Dad patted me on the back. "Okay, then. Let's go inside and get some breakfast."

Arthur returned to the cabin a few minutes later. He stamped the snow off his boots, glaring at me.

"You think you're funny," he muttered. "But wait till you see the snowman. Will you be laughing then?"

I swallowed hard.

The answer to his question was no. Definitely no.

After breakfast we hitched the dogs to the sled and set off for the snow rise. Arthur wouldn't talk to me and would hardly look at me. I guess he was angry about my joke.

Everybody else has forgiven me, I thought. Why won't he?

Nicole and I walked at the front of the sled with the dogs. Behind me I heard Dad's camera clicking furiously. I knew that meant he'd found something good to photograph. I turned round.

A large herd of elk moved towards us, towards the snow rise. We stopped to watch them.

"Look at them," Dad whispered. "Amazing." He quickly loaded new film into his camera and started snapping away again.

The elk calmly picked their way across the snow, antlers high. They stopped to eat at a stand of bushes. Arthur pulled back the rein on the lead sled-dog to keep him from barking.

Suddenly, one elk lifted its head. It seemed to sense something.

The other elk tensed up, too. Then they turned and began to gallop away across the tundra. Their hooves thundered over the snow.

Dad let his camera fall against his chest. "That's strange," he said. "I wonder what happened."

"Something scared them," Arthur said grimly. "It wasn't us. And it wasn't the dogs."

Dad scanned the horizon. "What was it, then?"

We all waited for Arthur's answer. But he only said, "We ought to turn around and head back to town right now."

"We're not going back," Dad insisted. "Not after coming all this way."

Arthur stared at him. "Are you going to take my advice or not?"

"No," Dad replied. "I've got a job to do here. And I've hired you to do a job. We're not going back without a good reason."

"We've *got* a good reason," Arthur insisted. "Only you won't see it that way."

"Push ahead," Dad ordered.

Arthur frowned and shouted "Mush!" to the dogs. The sled began to move. We followed it, on towards the snow rise.

Nicole walked a few feet ahead of me. I picked up a pile of snow and patted it into a ball. But then I thought I'd better not throw it. No one

172

seemed to be in the mood for snowball fights.

We marched through the snow for a couple of hours. I slipped off my gloves and wiggled my fingers. Frost kept collecting on my upper lip. I wiped it away.

We reached a stand of pine trees at the base of the snow rise. Suddenly the dogs stopped short. They began to bark.

"Mush!" Arthur shouted.

The dogs refused to go any further.

Nicole ran up to her favourite dog, Lars. "What is it, Lars? What's the matter?"

Lars howled.

"What's wrong with them?" Dad asked Arthur.

Arthur's face paled again. His hands shook. He stared intently into the trees, squinting into the brightness.

"Something's frightened the dogs," he said. "Look how their fur stands on end."

I patted Lars. It was true. His fur stood straight up. The dog growled.

"Not much scares these dogs," Arthur said. "Whatever it is, it's scaring them very badly."

The dogs all howled.

Nicole huddled close to Dad.

"There's something dangerous on that snow rise," Arthur said. "Something dangerous—and very near."

"I'm warning you, Mr Blake," Arthur said. "We've got to go back."

"No way," Dad protested. "We're not going back. I mean it."

The dogs barked and skittered nervously. Arthur shook his head. "I won't go any further. The dogs won't, either."

Dad shouted, "Mush!" to the dogs. They howled and started backing up.

"Mush!" he cried again. Instead of going forward, the dogs tried to turn around in the snow.

"You're upsetting them," Arthur said. "They won't go any further—I told you that."

"If we turn around now," Arthur added, "we can make it back to the cabin before it gets too late."

"What are we going to do, Dad?" I asked.

Dad frowned. "Maybe Arthur's right. Something is definitely frightening the dogs. There could be a bear or something nearby."

"Not a bear, Mr Blake," Arthur insisted. "These dogs are spooked. And so am I."

He marched away across the snow, heading back towards the musher's cabin.

"Arthur!" Dad called. "Come back here!"

Arthur didn't turn around. He didn't say a word. He just kept walking.

He must be really scared, I thought. And that sent a chill of fear down my back.

Still barking excitedly, the dogs pulled the sled around and started following Arthur.

Dad peered into the woods. "I wish I could see what's out there."

"Let's go and check it out," I urged. "Whatever it is, it'll probably make a great photo." That usually gets Dad.

He glanced back at Arthur, the dogs, and the sled, rushing towards the cabin. "No—it's too dangerous. We have no choice. Let's go, kids."

We trudged back to the cabin. "Maybe I can persuade Arthur to push on tomorrow," Dad muttered.

I didn't say anything. But I had a feeling it wouldn't be easy to get Arthur to climb that snow rise.

And maybe Arthur was right, I thought. Those dogs really were scared. It was definitely creepy.

Arthur was unhitching the dogs from the sled

when we reached the cabin. The dogs had calmed down a lot.

I yanked off my rucksack and collapsed on top of my sleeping bag.

"We might as well eat supper," Dad grumbled. I could tell he was in a terrible mood. "Jordan— why don't you and Nicole go and gather some firewood. But be careful."

"We will, Dad," Nicole promised.

I stood up and started out of the cabin.

"Jordan!" Dad scolded. "Put your knapsack on. I don't want you going *anywhere* without it. Understood?"

"We're just going for firewood," I protested. "I'm tired of carrying it. We'll only be gone a few minutes—and anyway, Nicole is wearing hers."

"No arguments," Dad snapped. "If you get lost, that food could keep you alive until we find you. You leave this cabin, you wear that knapsack. Is that clear?"

Boy, was he in a bad mood. "It's clear," I said, strapping on my pack.

Nicole and I crunched across the snow to the nearest trees. They lined a snow ridge about half a mile away.

We climbed the snow ridge. I made it to the top first.

"Nicole—look!"

On the other side of the snow ridge, I saw a

frozen stream. The first water we'd seen since we'd set out.

Nicole and I slid down the ridge and stared into the icy stream. I tested the ice with my foot.

"Don't step on it, Jordan!" Nicole cried. "You might fall in."

I tapped the ice with the tip of my boot. "It's solid," I told her.

"Still," Nicole said. "Don't take any chances. Dad will kill you if you have another accident."

"I wonder if there are fish swimming under there," I said, staring into the ice.

"We should tell Dad about this," Nicole said. "He might want to photograph it."

We left the stream to gather dead branches under the trees. We lugged them over the snow ridge and back across the snow to the cabin.

"Thanks, kids," Dad said when we burst into the cabin. He took the wood from us and started a fire in the stove. "How about pancakes for supper tonight?"

He's in a better mood now, I thought with relief.

Nicole told Dad about the frozen stream.

"Interesting," Dad said. "I'll take a look at it after supper. I've got to find *something* to photograph besides all this ice and snow."

The pancakes cheered all of us up—except for Arthur.

177

He ate a lot, but he didn't say much. He appeared jittery. He dropped his fork on the floor. Muttering to himself, he picked it up and started eating without wiping it off.

When supper was over, Nicole and I helped Dad clean up.

We were gathering up the supplies when the dogs started to bark.

I saw Arthur freeze.

"What's that?" I cried. "What's upset the dogs?"

The dogs yelped and barked.

Was someone out there?

An animal? A monster?

"I'll go and check," Arthur said solemnly. He pulled on his coat and wool cap and hurried out of the cabin.

Dad grabbed his coat. "Stay here," he instructed Nicole and me. He followed Arthur.

We stared at each other, listening to the yelping dogs. A few seconds later, the barking stopped.

Dad poked his head back into the cabin. "Nothing out there. We don't know what got them upset. But Arthur is calming them down."

Dad grabbed his camera. "You two get some sleep, okay? I'm going to check out that stream. I won't be gone long."

He draped the camera over his fur coat collar. The cabin door slammed behind him.

We heard Dad's footsteps crunching over the

snow. Then silence. Nicole and I climbed into our sleeping bags.

I rolled on to my side, trying to get comfortable. It was after eight o'clock, but still light outside. The sun filtered through the window of the cabin.

The light reminded me of when I was little. Mum used to try to make me take a nap in the afternoon. I never could sleep in the daytime.

I closed my eyes. I opened them. I wasn't sleepy.

I turned my head and glanced at Nicole. She lay on her back, her eyes wide open.

"I can't sleep," I announced.

"Me neither," she replied.

I squirmed in my sleeping bag.

"Where's Arthur?" Nicole asked. "I wonder what's taking him so long?"

"I guess he's hanging out with the dogs," I said. "I think he likes them better than he likes us."

"That's for sure," Nicole agreed.

We tossed and turned some more. The sky stayed bright. The light poured in through the cabin window.

"I give up," I groaned. "Let's go outside and build a snowman or something."

"Dad said to stay put."

"We won't go anywhere. We'll stay by the cabin," I assured her.

I crawled out of my sleeping bag and started getting dressed. Nicole sat up.

"We shouldn't," she warned.

"Come on. What could happen?"

She stood up and pulled on her jumper. "If I don't do something, I'll go stir-crazy," she admitted.

We bundled up. I pulled open the cabin door.

"Jordan—wait!" Nicole cried. "You forgot your knapsack."

"We're just going outside the door," I complained.

"Come on. Dad said we have to. He'll be furious if he finds us outside. And he'll be even more furious if you're not wearing your pack."

"Oh, all right," I grumbled. I hoisted the pack over my shoulders. "Like something's really going to happen to us."

We stepped out into the cold. I kicked at the snow.

Nicole grabbed my coat sleeve. "Listen!" she whispered.

We heard the crunch of footsteps behind the cabin. "It's Arthur," I told her.

We crept around to the back. It *was* Arthur.

He crouched beside the dog-sled, hitching up one of the dogs. Two others were already tied to the sled.

"Arthur!" I cried. "What's up?"

Startled, he turned to us. He didn't reply. Instead, he jumped on the back of the sled.

"Mush!" he commanded the dogs at the top of his lungs.

The dogs leaned forward, tugging hard. The sled began to slide away.

"Arthur! Where are you going?" I screamed. "Come back!"

The sled picked up speed.

"Arthur! Arthur!" Nicole and I ran after him, shouting his name.

But the sled raced further and further away from us.

Arthur never turned back.

Nicole and I chased after the sled, watching it grow tinier and tinier.

"Arthur! Come back!"

"He's got our food!" I cried.

We couldn't let him get away. We ran as fast as we could, our boots falling deep into the snow.

The sled climbed over a tall ridge of snow.

"Stop! Stop!" Nicole screamed. "Please!"

"We can't keep up with the dogs," I gasped.

"We have to try," Nicole cried frantically. "We can't let Arthur leave us here!"

The sled disappeared over the top of the ridge. We clawed our way up. The snow slid under our feet.

By the time we had reached the top, Arthur and the dogs were far ahead of us. We watched in horror as they quickly disappeared across the tundra.

Exhausted, I collapsed in the snow. "They're getting away," I choked out.

"Jordan, get up!" Nicole pleaded.

"We can't catch him," I moaned.

Then Nicole said in a small voice, "Where are we?"

I stood up and gazed around. Snow, snow, snow. All around us, nothing but snow. No landmarks. No sign of the cabin.

Clouds had covered the sun. The wind picked up. Snow began to fall.

I had no idea where we were.

"Which way is the cabin?" I asked in a shrill voice. "Which way did we come?"

We scanned the horizon through the falling snow. I didn't see the cabin anywhere.

Nicole tugged on my arm. "The cabin is that way. Let's go!"

"No!" The snow came down harder and faster, stinging my eyes. I shouted into the wind. "The cabin's the other way! That's not the way we came."

"Look!" Nicole yelled, pointing down. "Our tracks! We'll just follow them home."

We started down the ridge, following the ruts we'd made in the snow. The wind howled, growing stronger.

We followed our own footprints for a short while. It was so hard to see in the falling snow. All white and grey. The whole world. White and grey.

Nicole peered at me through the thick curtain of snow. "I can hardly see you!" she shouted.

We crouched low, searching for our footprints.

"They're gone!" I cried. The snow had already covered them up.

Nicole clutched my arm. "Jordan, I'm getting scared."

I was getting scared, too. But I didn't tell Nicole.

"We'll find the cabin," I assured her. "Don't worry. I bet Dad's looking for us right now."

I wished I believed it myself. The wind pelted us with hard, icy snow. I squinted into the wind. Nothing but white. White on white. White on grey.

"Don't let go of me!" I shouted to Nicole.

"What?"

"I said, don't let go of me! We could easily lose each other in the storm!"

She tightened her grip on my arm to show she understood.

"I'm so cold," she shouted. "Let's run!"

We tried to run through the snow, stumbling against the wind. "Dad!" we called out. "Dad!"

I had no idea where we were going—but I knew we had to go somewhere.

"Look!" Nicole cried, pointing through the thick snow. "I think I see something!"

I stared as hard as I could, but I didn't see anything.

Nicole pulled me along. "Come on!" she shouted.

We ran blindly. Suddenly, the ground gave way under our feet.

Still holding on to Nicole, I felt myself being sucked down under the snow.

Down we fell. Down into the freezing white.

The snow rushed up, swirled around us.

And buried us.

Another crevasse, I thought. Another deep pit in the snow.

Much deeper than the first.

We both cried out as we landed. Tangled up in each other.

"Get off!" Nicole shrieked. "Where are we? Get off!"

Feeling dazed, I struggled to my feet. Then I grabbed both of her hands and tugged her up.

"Oh no," Nicole groaned.

We both stared up to the top. I could barely make out the grey of the sky, high above our heads.

And all around us, high walls of snow. Powdery snow that blew down on us. I peered up to the top of the pit. Chunks of snow broke off the

187

icy walls. They made soft *thuds* as they landed beside us on the snowy pit floor.

"We're trapped down here!" Nicole wailed. "Dad will never find us. Never!"

I grabbed the shoulders of her coat. A chunk of snow fell off the pit wall and landed on top of my boots. "Try to stay calm," I told her. But my voice trembled as I said it.

"Calm? How can I stay calm?" she demanded shrilly.

"Dad will find us," I said. I wasn't sure I believed it. I swallowed hard, trying to fight down my panic.

"Daaaaaad!" Nicole screamed. She cupped her hands around her mouth, raised her head towards the sky, and screamed at the top of her lungs. "Daaaaaaad! *Daaaaaaaaad!*"

I clapped a glove over her mouth.

Too late.

I heard a low rumbling.

The rumbling became a roar as the snow walls began to crack and crumble.

Crumble down. Down on us.

Trembling with horror, I knew what was happening.

Nicole had started an avalanche.

As sheets of snow tumbled down on us, I grabbed Nicole.

I pushed her against the pit wall. Then I flattened myself against the wall, too.

The snow roared down.

I pressed myself tight against the wall—and to my shock, the wall gave way!

"Aaaah!" I let out a startled cry. Nicole and I tumbled through the side of the pit.

We stumbled forward into total darkness.

I heard a crash behind us. My heart pounding, I turned in time to see the pit fill up. Snow piled over the opening in the wall.

Nicole and I were sealed in. Shut in this dark hole.

Our way out was gone. The pit was gone.

We crouched in the dark tunnel-like opening, trembling, gasping in fright.

"Where are we?" Nicole choked out. "What do we do now?"

189

"I don't know." I grabbed the wall. We seemed to be in a narrow passageway. The walls around us were made of rock instead of snow.

My eyes adjusted to the darkness. I could see a dim light at the end of the passageway.

"Let's see what's down there," I urged Nicole.

We crawled on our hands and knees through the passage towards the light. The passage ended. We stood up.

We found ourselves in a big cave. The top of the cave towered high above our heads. Water trickled slowly down one of the walls. A dim glow came from somewhere near the back.

"The light must be coming from outside," Nicole said. "That means there's a way out of here."

We crept slowly through the cave. The only sound I could hear was the *drip, drip, drip* of melting icicles.

Soon we'll be out of here, I thought.

"Jordan," Nicole whispered. "Look!"

On the floor of the cave I could make out a footprint. A gigantic footprint. Bigger than the fake one I'd made in the snow that morning.

Five of my shoes could fit inside that footprint.

I took a few steps—and saw another footprint.

Nicole grabbed my arm.

"Do you think it's. . . ?" She stopped.

I knew what she was thinking.

We traced the giant footprints across the cave

floor. They led us straight to a shadowy corner in the back—and stopped.

I glanced up.

Nicole gasped.

We both saw it at the same time.

The creature.

The Abominable Snowman!

He loomed over us.

He stood upright like a human, covered in brown fur. Black eyes stared out of an ugly face, half-human, half-gorilla.

He wasn't that tall—about a head taller than me—but he seemed huge. His body was thick and powerful, with gigantic feet and fur-covered hands—as big as baseball gloves.

"We're t-trapped!" Nicole stammered.

She was right.

The entrance behind us had been blocked by the avalanche. There was no way we could slip past this giant creature.

No way.

The Abominable Snowman glared down at us. Then it started to move.

My teeth began to chatter.

I squeezed my eyes shut and trembled, waiting for the monster to grab us.

A second passed. Then another.

Nothing happened.

I opened my eyes. The snowman hadn't moved.

Nicole took a step forward. "He's frozen!" she cried.

I blinked in the dim light. "Huh?" It was true. The snowman stood frozen in a huge block of clear ice.

I touched the ice. The monster stood inside it like a statue.

"If he's frozen in ice," I wondered, "then what made those giant footprints?"

Nicole bent down to study the prints. She shuddered again at their huge size.

"They lead right to the block of ice," she

declared. "The snowman must have made them somehow."

"Maybe he walked back here and accidentally froze," I suggested. I touched the back wall of the cave, where icy water dripped from above.

"Or maybe he goes into the ice to rest," I added. "Like Dracula going to sleep in his coffin at dawn."

I backed away. It was too frightening, being this close to him. But the monster stayed perfectly still under the thick ice.

Nicole leaned close to the ice. "Look at his hands!" she cried. "Or paws, or whatever."

Like the rest of his body, his hands were covered with brown fur. He had thick fingers, like a man's. Jutting out of them were long, sharp claws.

A chill ran down my spine at the sight of those claws. What did he use them for? Ripping wild animals to pieces? Tearing up people who got in his way?

He had powerful legs, with shorter claws on his toes. I studied his face. Fur covered his whole head, except for a circle of hairless skin around his eyes, nose, and mouth. The skin was a pinkish red. His lips were thick and white and set in a mean-looking grimace.

"He's definitely a mammal," Nicole declared. "The fur is a dead giveaway."

I rolled my eyes. "This is no time for biology

lessons, Nicole. Wait until Dad sees this. He'll go crazy! If he can get a picture of this, he'll be famous!"

"Yeah," Nicole sighed. "If we can find Dad. If we ever get out of here."

"There's got to be a way out," I said. I moved to a side wall and pressed it with my hands, searching for a hole, a chink in the rock, anything.

After a few minutes I found a tiny crack. "Nicole!" I cried. "I found something!"

She raced to my side. I pointed out the crack in the cave wall. She frowned with disappointment.

"That's just a crack," she said.

"You don't know everything," I protested. "Maybe there's a secret door here. A hidden passage. Or something."

She sighed. "I guess it's worth a shot."

We pressed on the crack. We stuck our fingers into it. We kicked it. I even tried karate-chopping it.

Nothing.

"I hate to break this to you, Jordan," she said. "But I was right. As always. All you found was a crack in the wall."

"Well, keep looking," I snarled. "We've got to get out of here!"

I kept searching. I ran my hands along the wall, my back to the monster.

Suddenly I heard a noise. A loud *crack!*

"Nicole!" I cried. "Did you find something?"

I whirled around. I realized Nicole hadn't made that sound. She stared at the monster in horror.

"What?" I asked her. "What's wrong?"

I heard another *crack!*

"The ice is cracking!" Nicole screamed. "The monster—he's breaking out!"

Crack!

The block of ice splintered apart. Nicole and I pressed ourselves against a wall, watching in horror.

The Abominable Snowman burst from the ice. Chunks of ice smashed on the floor and shattered like glass. The snowman shook himself, growling like a wolf.

"Run!" I screamed.

Nicole and I took off. But there was nowhere to go. We stumbled to the other side of the cave—as far away from the monster as we could get.

"The passageway!" I cried. I ducked down and started to crawl through the passage.

Nicole grabbed me.

"Wait! It's blocked! The avalanche— remember?"

Yes. Of course. The way out of the cave was blocked by tons of snow.

196

Across the cave, the monster uttered a ferocious roar that shook the walls.

Nicole and I cowered in a corner of the cave. I felt her trembling next to me.

"Maybe he didn't see us," I whispered.

"Then why is he roaring?" Nicole whispered back.

The monster twitched his gorilla nose in the air, sniffing.

Oh, no! I thought. Can he smell us from across the cave?

He turned his huge, furry head one way and then the other.

He's searching for us, I realized. He smells us.

"Uh!" he grunted. He stared into a corner of the cave—our corner of the cave.

"Uh!" he grunted again.

"Oh, no!" Nicole moaned. "He can see us!"

The big creature staggered towards us, grunting with each heavy step.

I pressed myself against the cave wall, wishing the cave would swallow us up.

Anything would be better than having *him* swallow us!

The monster kept coming. His footsteps shook the floor of the cave. *Boom, boom, boom.*

We huddled on the floor. We tried to make ourselves as small as we could.

He stopped inches in front of us and roared again. A deafening roar.

"His teeth!" Nicole cried.

I saw them, too. Two rows of huge, razor-sharp teeth.

The monster growled.

And reached for us. His sharp claws flashed.

He swiped at me. I tried to duck away.

The monster snarled in frustration. He reached out again. . .

He clamped a powerful paw on Nicole's head.

"Help!" Nicole screamed. "He's crushing me!"

"Let go of her!" I shrieked.

But I knew I was helpless.

The Abominable Snowman growled and turned Nicole around roughly.

Then he reached behind her and grabbed her knapsack. He ripped it off her shoulder with a sharp, hard tug.

"Hey!" I cried in horror.

With one claw he sliced open the canvas knapsack. He reached inside. And pulled something out.

A bag. A bag of trail mix.

Nicole and I stared in amazement as he poured the trail mix into his mouth.

"Weird," I choked out. "He likes trail mix."

The monster crumpled up the bag and shifted through Nicole's pack, searching for more.

"That's all there is," Nicole whispered to me.

With an angry growl, the monster tossed Nicole's pack away.

199

"Now what?" Nicole whispered.

I reached into my own knapsack, and with a trembling hand I yanked out my bag of trail mix. I heaved it at the monster.

The bag hit the floor and slid to the monster's feet. He bent down. Grabbed it. Tore it open. And hungrily gulped down the trail mix.

When he finished, I shoved my bag towards him.

He grunted. Then he dumped out my stuff.

No more trail mix.

Uh-oh.

The monster stretched and roared. Then he reached down. With two gigantic arms, he grabbed Nicole and me.

He lifted us up.

He raised us towards his face.

Towards his mouth.

Preparing to eat us.

I struggled, but he was too strong. I pounded my fists on his chest. I kicked as hard as I could. He didn't seem to feel it.

He clutched Nicole and me like a couple of dolls.

"Please don't eat us!" I begged. "Please!"

The monster grunted. He draped us both over the crook of one arm. Then he staggered back across the cave, gripping us tightly.

I kicked him in the side. No reaction. Nothing.

"Let go!" I shrieked. "Let us down!"

"Where's he taking us?" Nicole cried, bouncing as the creature tramped across the cave.

Maybe he wants to roast us, I thought grimly. Maybe he doesn't like his kids raw.

He lugged us to the back of the cave. With one powerful swipe of the paw, he knocked a boulder aside. A narrow passage appeared behind it.

Nicole moaned. "Why didn't we see that before? Maybe we could have escaped!"

"Too late now," I groaned.

The snowman pulled us through the passage. We came out into a smaller cave, flooded with light. I glanced up.

Above us I could see the grey sky.

A way out!

Balancing us in one arm, the monster scaled the wall of the cave. With big, lurching steps, he climbed out of the hole.

Cold air blasted me in the face. But the monster's body pulsed with heat.

The blizzard had stopped. Fresh snow covered the tundra.

The monster stumbled through the snow, grunting as he walked.

His gigantic feet sank deep into the snow. But with each huge step he covered a lot of ground.

Where was he taking us? Where?

Maybe he has another cave, I thought with a shudder. A cave with more monsters in it. His friends. They'll all feast on us!

I tried again to break out of the snowman's grip. I kicked and squirmed as hard as I could.

The monster growled. He dug his claws into my side.

"Ow!" I yelped. But I stopped squirming. If I moved, his claws dug deeper.

Poor Dad, I thought sadly. He'll never know what happened to us.

Unless he finds our bones buried in the snow.

Suddenly, I heard barking. A dog!

The Abominable Snowman stopped. He growled and sniffed the air. Then he gently dropped Nicole and me in the snow.

We landed unsteadily on our feet.

Nicole stared at me in surprise.

We started to run, stumbling through the deep snow. I glanced back.

"Is he chasing us?" Nicole asked.

I couldn't be sure. I couldn't see him now. I only saw white.

"Keep running!" I shouted.

Then I saw something familiar in the distance. A brown speck.

I bumped Nicole. "The cabin!"

We ran even faster. If we could just get to the cabin. . .

From the cabin we heard furious barking— the dog Arthur had left behind.

"Dad! Dad!" we shrieked. We burst through the door. "We found him! We found the Abominable Snowman!"

"Dad?"

The cabin stood empty. Empty and bare.

Dad was gone.

My eyes darted around the empty cabin.

"Dad? Dad?"

My heart skipped a beat. My throat went dry.

Where did he go?

Was he out searching for Nicole and me? Did he get lost in the snow?

"We—we're all alone," I murmured.

Nicole and I ran to the window. A thin layer of snow frosted the pane. We peered out into the bright sunlight.

No sign of Dad.

"At least the snowman didn't follow us," I said.

"Jordan, why did he let us go?" Nicole asked softly.

"I think the barking dog scared him," I replied.

If that dog hadn't barked, what would the monster have done to us?

As the question pushed into my mind, I heard

the dog start to bark again. Nicole and I both gasped.

"The snowman—!" I cried. "He's back! Hide!"

We glanced around, frantically searching for a good hiding place. The cabin was so bare—it wouldn't take the monster long to find us.

"Behind the stove!" Nicole urged.

We dashed to the small, square stove and crouched behind it.

Outside the cabin we heard the slow, heavy footsteps of the monster.

Crunch, crunch, crunch. Footsteps over the snow.

Nicole grabbed my hand. We froze, waiting. Listening.

Crunch, crunch.

Please don't come into the cabin, I prayed. Please don't capture us again.

The footsteps stopped outside the door. I squeezed my eyes shut.

The door burst open. A blast of cold air blew into the room.

"Jordan? Nicole?"

Dad!

We jumped out from behind the stove. There stood Dad, with his camera around his neck.

We both ran to him and hugged him. "Dad! I'm so glad it's you!"

"Hi!" he replied. "What's going on, guys? I

205

expected you to be asleep." He glanced around the cabin. "Hey—where's Arthur?"

"He took off!" I cried breathlessly. "He took the sled. He took all the food and three of the dogs."

"We chased after him," Nicole added. "But he got away."

Dad's face filled with surprise, then horror. "I'd better radio for help. We won't last long without food."

"Dad—listen." I blocked his way to the radio. "Nicole and I—we found the Abominable Snowman!"

He sidestepped around me. "This is no time for jokes, Jordan. If we don't get help, we could starve to death out here!"

"He's not joking, Dad," Nicole insisted, tugging Dad's arm. "We really found the snowman. He lives in a cave under the snow."

Dad stopped and studied Nicole. He always believes her. But this time he wasn't sure.

"It's true!" I cried. "Come on—we'll show you!"

Nicole and I tugged him out the door.

"Jordan, if this is one of your tricks, you are going to be in *major* trouble," he warned. "We're in a serious situation here and—"

"Dad, he's not kidding!" Nicole cried impatiently. "Come on!"

We led him out into the snow to the spot where

206

the snowman had dropped us. We pointed out his huge footprints.

"Why should I believe this?" Dad said. "You faked the snowman's footprints this morning, Jordan. These just look a little bigger."

"Dad, I swear—I didn't make these prints!"

"We'll show you the cave, Dad," Nicole promised. "Follow the footprints. You'll see. It's unbelievable!"

I knew Dad went along with us only because Nicole insisted. He trusted her. She never played jokes on him.

Leaning into the wind, we traced the giant prints across the snow. Dad couldn't resist snapping pictures of them—just in case.

The footsteps led us back to the cave. They stopped at an opening in the ground.

"The cave is down that hole," I told Dad, pointing.

I think Dad believed us now. "Let's go. Check it out," he said.

"Huh?" I cried. "Back down there? To the monster?"

Dad was already sliding down to the cave opening. He reached up to help Nicole climb down.

I hesitated. "Dad—wait. You don't understand. There's a monster down there!"

"Come on, Jordan," Dad urged. "I want to see this for myself."

I had no choice. Dad was going in there no matter what I said. And I didn't want to wait outside alone. I scrambled down to the opening of the cave.

The three of us felt our way along the narrow passage until we reached the mouth of the big cave.

Keeping close together, Dad and Nicole walked in. But I stopped at the entrance and stared into the cave.

"Jordan! Come on!" Dad whispered.

There's a monster in there, I thought with a shudder. A huge monster with long claws and sharp teeth.

We managed to escape from him once. Why are we going back? What's going to happen to us in there?

I had a bad feeling. A very bad feeling.

Dad grabbed me by the hand and pulled me into the cave. I heard the drip of icy water against the back wall. I blinked in the darkness.

Where was he? Where was the Abominable Snowman?

I heard Dad's camera clicking away. I tried to stay close to Dad. I cried out when I spotted the snowman. I expected him to roar and lumber after us.

But he stood stiffly, staring straight ahead.

Refrozen again. Inside a huge block of ice.

Nicole stepped closer to the block of ice. "How does he do that?"

"This is *amazing*!" Dad cried, snapping picture after picture. "*Incredible!*"

I stared up at the monster's face. He glared out at us from inside the ice. His black eyes glittered, his mouth set in a toothy snarl.

"This is the most amazing discovery in

209

history!" Dad exclaimed. "Do you realize how famous we are going to be?"

He stopped shooting for a second and peered up at the brown-furred monster.

"Why stop here?" he murmured. "Why go home with nothing but photos? Why not take the snowman himself back to California? Do you know what a sensation that will create?"

"But—how?" Nicole asked.

"He's alive, you know, Dad," I warned. "I mean, he can crack out of that ice. And when he does, it's really scary. I don't think you could control him."

Dad knocked gently on the ice, testing it. "We won't let him out of the ice," he said. "At least not until we've got him under control."

Dad walked all the way around the block of ice, rubbing his chin. "If we cut the ice a bit, it might fit into the supply trunk," he said. "Then we could carry the snowman back to California in the block of ice, locked in the trunk. It's airtight, so the ice won't melt."

He stepped up close to the ice and snapped a few more shots of the snowman's snarling face. "Let's go and get the trunk, kids."

"Dad—wait." I didn't like this idea. "You don't understand. The snowman could *rush* us! He let us go once. But why take another chance?"

"Look at his teeth, Dad," Nicole pleaded. "He's so strong, he picked us both up at once!"

"It's worth the risk," Dad insisted. "Neither of you is hurt, right?"

Nicole and I nodded. "Yes, but—"

"Let's go." Dad had made his mind up. He wasn't going to listen to our warnings.

I'd never seen him so excited. As we hurried from the cave, he called to the snowman, "Don't go away—we'll be right back!"

We rushed over the snow to the cabin. Dad pulled the supply trunk outside. It was about six feet long and three feet wide.

"The snowman will fit," he said. "But with him inside the trunk, it will be very heavy."

"We need the dog-sled to pull it," Nicole said.

"But Arthur took the sled," I reminded them. "So I guess the deal is off. We'll just have to go home without an Abominable Snowman. Too bad!"

"Maybe there's another sled around somewhere," Dad suggested. "This is an old musher's cabin, after all."

I remembered the old sled I'd seen in the dog shed. Nicole had seen it, too. She led Dad to it.

"Fantastic!" Dad cried. "Now let's go and get that snowman before he escapes."

We hitched Lars, our only dog, to the old sled and towed the supply trunk to the cave.

Then we crept silently to the cave, pulling the

trunk behind us. "Careful, Dad," I warned. "He might have broken out of the ice by now."

But the Abominable Snowman stood where we'd left him, frozen in his block of ice.

Dad began to cut the ice down to size with a hacksaw.

I paced nervously. "Hurry!" I whispered. "He could burst out any minute!"

"This isn't easy," Dad snapped. "I'm working as fast as I can." He hacked away.

Each second felt like an hour to me. I watched the snowman carefully for any signs of movement.

"Dad, do you have to saw so loudly?" I complained. "The noise could wake him up!"

"Relax, Jordan," Dad said. But his voice was tight and shrill, too.

Then I heard a *crack*.

"Look out!" I cried. "He's breaking out!"

Dad straightened up. "*I* cracked the ice a bit, Jordan."

I studied the monster. He hadn't moved.

"Okay, kids," Dad said. "We're ready." Dad had cut the ice into a six-foot-long rectangle. "Help me slide this into the trunk."

I opened the lid of the trunk. Nicole and I helped Dad tip the ice over and gently drop it into the trunk. It just barely fitted.

We slid the trunk along the ground to the opening of the cave. Dad tied a rope around it and climbed out of the hole. "I'll tie the rope to the sled," Dad called from above. "That way Lars can help me hoist it out."

"Hey," I whispered to Nicole, "let's sneak some snowballs into the trunk—just for fun. We can throw them at Kyle and Kara when we get home. Snow from the cave of the Abominable Snowman—they'll never top that!"

"No—please. Don't open the trunk," Nicole begged. "We just barely got the snowman inside."

"We can squeeze a few snowballs in," I insisted. I quickly made a bunch of snowballs, packing them tight. Then I cracked open the trunk and slipped them inside, next to the block of ice.

I checked the monster one last time for signs of life. The ice was solid. We were safe.

"They won't melt in there," I said, sealing the lid of the trunk shut. We locked it with the bolt and tightened the rope around it. I felt pretty sure the snowman wouldn't be able to break out of there, even if he did crack through the ice.

"Ready?" Dad shouted from up above. "One, two, three—*heave!*"

Dad and Lars tugged on the rope until the chest lifted off the ground. Nicole and I squatted beneath it to help push it up.

"Again!" Dad yelled. "Heave!"

We pushed as hard as we could. "It's so heavy!" Nicole complained.

"Come on, kids!" Dad called. "Push!"

We gave the trunk a shove. Dad and Lars tugged it over the lip of the cave opening.

Dad collapsed in the snow. "Whew," he muttered, wiping his brow. "Well, the hardest part is over."

He helped Nicole and me scramble out.

We all rested a few minutes. Then we dragged the trunk on to the sledge. Dad secured it with the rope. Lars pulled the sledge back to the cabin.

Once inside, Dad hugged us both. "What a day! What a great day!"

He turned to me. "See, Jordan? Nothing terrible happened."

"We're lucky," I said.

"I'm so sleepy," Nicole complained, sinking on to her sleeping bag.

I glanced out of the window. The sun sat high in the sky, as usual. But I knew it had to be very late.

Dad glanced at his watch. "It's almost midnight. You two should get some sleep." He frowned. "I'd hate to wake up here in the morning with no food, though. I'm going to radio for help. You guys can sleep when we get back to town."

"Can we stay in a hotel?" I asked Dad. "In a bed?"

"If we can find one," he promised. He opened his pack, searching for the radio.

He shuffled stuff around in his pack. Then he pulled things out, one by one. A compass. An extra camera. Cans of film. A pair of socks, rolled up.

I didn't like the look on his face. He turned the pack over and dumped everything on the floor. He sifted through it again, getting frantic.

"Dad? What's the matter?"

When he turned to me, he had a terrified expression on his face. "The radio," he murmured. "It's gone."

"No!" Nicole and I both shrieked.

"I don't believe it!" Dad cried, pounding his fist against his empty pack. "Arthur must have taken the radio so we wouldn't report him."

I stomped around the room, frightened and furious. Our dogs, our sled, our food—Arthur had taken them all.

And now the radio.

Did Arthur leave us here to freeze? To starve?

"Calm down, Jordan," Dad said.

"But, Dad—" Nicole interrupted.

Dad shushed her. "Just a second, Nicole. I've got to think of a way out of this." Dad searched the cabin. "Don't panic. Don't panic. Don't panic," he instructed himself.

"But Dad—" Nicole said, tugging at his sleeve.

"Nicole!" I snapped. "We're in huge trouble. We could die out here!"

"Dad!" she insisted. "Listen to me! You

wrapped up the radio last night so it wouldn't freeze. It's in your sleeping bag!"

Dad's mouth dropped open. "You're right!" he cried. He hurried to his sleeping bag and reached inside. He dug into his sleeping bag— and pulled out the radio, wrapped in a woollen scarf.

He switched on the radio and fiddled with the dials. "Iknek, Iknek. Come in, Iknek."

Dad asked the Iknek airport to send us a helicopter. He tried to describe where we were.

Nicole and I smiled sleepily at each other.

"We're going home!" she said happily. "Home to sunny, hot Pasadena."

"I'm going to kiss a palm tree!" I declared. "I never want to see snow again."

I had no idea that our snowy adventure was just beginning!

"Ahhhh!" I sighed. "Feel that sun? Nice and hot."

"The radio said it's a hundred degrees today," Nicole reported.

"I love it!" I beamed. "Love it!"

I slapped more tanning lotion on my chest.

Our Alaska trip all seemed unreal, now that we were home in Pasadena. The cold, the snow, the wind blowing over the rolling white tundra. The snarling, brown-furred Abominable Snowman. It all seemed like a dream.

But I knew it was no dream.

Dad had hidden the trunk with the Abominable Snowman inside the darkroom in the back garden. Every time I passed it, I remembered the trip ... remembered the creature lying frozen in there—and shivered.

In our swimsuits, Nicole and I caught some rays in the back garden. Good old sunny Pasadena. Where it never, never snowed.

Thank goodness.

Lauren came over to hear about our trip. I wanted to tell her the *whole* story. But Dad told us to keep quiet about it—at least until the snowman was safely settled somewhere.

"I don't believe you two!" Lauren snorted. "A week ago you wouldn't shut up about snow. Now you're letting the sun burn you to a crisp!"

"Well, we did the cold thing and now we're doing the hot thing," I told her. "Anyway, I've seen enough snow to last me the rest of my life."

"Tell me about the trip," Lauren insisted. "Tell me everything!"

"It's a big secret," Nicole told her. She and I exchanged glances.

"Secret? What kind of secret?" Lauren demanded.

Before we could reply, Dad emerged from the darkroom. He squinted in the sunlight. He wore a down jacket, a ski cap and gloves. He had turned the air-conditioning way up in the darkroom and covered the trunk with ice packs, to keep the snowman cold.

"I'm going into the city now," he announced, removing his coat. Dad had a meeting with some scientists and wildlife experts in Los Angeles.

He wanted to turn the Abominable Snowman over to the right people. He wanted to be sure the snowman would be treated well.

219

"Are you kids going to be all right while I'm gone?" he asked.

"Of course," Nicole replied. "We survived the Alaskan tundra. I think we can live through one afternoon in our own back garden."

"My mum is at home," Lauren said. "She'll be around if we need anything."

"Good." Dad nodded. "Okay, I'm off. But remember—Jordan and Nicole, are you listening? Don't touch the supply trunk. Stay away from it—understood?"

"Gotcha, Dad," I promised.

"All right. I'll bring a pizza home for dinner."

"Good luck, Dad!" Nicole called. I watched him jump into the car and drive off.

"So what's the big secret?" Lauren asked as soon as Dad was gone. "What's in the supply trunk?"

Nicole and I glanced at each other.

"Come on. Spill," Lauren urged. "I won't leave you alone until you tell me."

I couldn't resist. I *had* to tell someone. "We found him. We found him and we brought him back."

"Found who?"

"The snowman!" Nicole exclaimed. "The Abominable Snowman!"

Lauren rolled her eyes. "For sure. And did you find the Tooth Fairy up there, too?"

"Yes, we did," I joked.

"He's lying in the darkroom right now," Nicole told Lauren.

Lauren's face twisted in confusion. "Who— the Tooth Fairy?"

"No. The Abominable Snowman. A real one," I said. "Trapped in a block of ice."

Along with four or five snowballs, I thought to myself.

Snowballs I could throw at Lauren. For a nice little surprise.

"Prove it," Lauren challenged us. "You're making it all up. You think you're really funny."

Nicole and I exchanged glances. I knew what she was thinking. Dad had just told us to stay away from the trunk.

"You two are as bad as the Miller twins," Lauren complained.

That did it. "Come on," I said. "We'll show you."

"We'd better not, Jordan," Nicole argued.

"We won't hurt anything," I promised. "We'll just pull open the lid a tiny bit so Lauren can see him. Then we'll slam it shut. No harm done."

I climbed off my lounge chair and started across the lawn to the darkroom. Nicole and Lauren followed me.

I knew they would.

I opened the darkroom door and switched on the light. A blast of cold air swept over me, making my bare chest tingle.

221

Nicole hesitated in the doorway. "Jordan, maybe we shouldn't."

"Oh, come on, Nicole," Lauren chided. "There's no Abominable Snowman. You two are ridiculous!"

"We're not ridiculous!" Nicole protested.

"We might as well show her, Nicole," I said.

Nicole didn't reply. She stepped into the darkroom and shut the door.

In my bathing suit, I was shivering from the cold. It was almost like being back in Alaska.

I knelt beside the huge trunk. I unhooked the latches.

Slowly, carefully, I lifted the heavy lid.

Peered inside.

And let out a chilling, bloodcurdling scream of horror.

Nicole and Lauren shrieked and leaped back.

Nicole backed into the wall with a *crash*.

Lauren ducked under the developing table.

I couldn't keep a straight face. I started to laugh. "Gotcha!" I cried gleefully. I was so pleased with myself.

I had scared them to death. They were both stiffer than the Abominable Snowman. He lay frozen and still inside his block of ice.

"Jordan—you creep!" Nicole declared angrily. She punched me in the back.

Lauren punched me too. Then she peered into the open trunk.

And let out another scream. "He's real! You— you weren't kidding!" I could see that she was breathing hard.

"It's okay, Lauren," I assured her. "He can't hurt you. He's frozen."

She stepped closer and stared down at him.

"He's huge!" she cried in amazement. "His—his eyes are open. They're so mean-looking!"

"Close the lid, Jordan," Nicole insisted. "Quick. We've seen enough."

"Now do you believe us?" I asked Lauren.

She nodded. "It's . . . awesome!" She shook her head, stunned at the amazing sight.

Before I shut the lid, I sneaked two snowballs out of the bottom of the trunk. Sniggering, I passed one to Nicole.

"What's so funny?" Lauren asked suspiciously.

"Nothing," I said. I sealed the lid shut and latched the trunk. That'll hold him, I thought. We're safe. Dad will never know we sneaked a peek at the monster.

We left the darkroom, closing the door carefully behind us.

"That creature is just so awesome!" Lauren exclaimed. "What is your dad going to do with him?"

"We're not sure yet," Nicole replied. "Dad's trying to figure that out."

She held her hands behind her back, hiding the snowball from Lauren. Suddenly she shouted, "Hey, Lauren! Think fast!"

She threw the snowball at Lauren. It missed. *Splat!* It hit a tree.

"Nice shot, ace!" I cried sarcastically.

But then I gaped at the tree in shock.

The snowball—it didn't crumble to the ground.

It started to *grow*!

Thick white snow spread quickly up the tree trunk— and over the branches. Within seconds, the entire tree was covered with snow!

"Wow!" Lauren gasped. "Nicole—how did you do that?"

Nicole and I stared open-mouthed at the snow-covered tree.

I was so stunned, the snowball fell out of my hand.

I jumped back as it hit the ground—and spread!

"Oh, wow!" I shrieked. I watched snow spread over the lawn like a white blanket.

It spread under our bare feet. Over the driveway. Out to the street.

"Ooooh! It's cold!" Nicole wailed, hopping from foot to foot.

"This is too weird!" I cried. "It's a hundred degrees out—and the snow isn't melting! It's spreading—and growing deeper!"

I turned to see Lauren hopping and dancing, whirling around wildly. "Snow! Snow!" she sang. "It's wonderful! Snow in Pasadena!"

"Jordan—" Nicole said quietly. "This isn't right. We should have left this snow in the cave. It isn't normal snow."

Of course she was right. Any cave where an

Abominable Snowman lives has got to be a weird place. But how could we have guessed—?

"Let's build a snowman!" Lauren cried gleefully.

"No!" Nicole warned. "Don't touch it. Don't do anything, Lauren. Not until we've figured this out."

I don't think Lauren heard my sister. She was too excited. She kicked a spray of snow at an evergreen bush. The bush froze over with snow.

"What are we going to do?" I asked Nicole. "What's going to happen when Dad comes home? He'll kill us!"

Nicole shrugged. "Beats me."

"But—but—you're supposed to be the *brain*!" I sputtered.

"This is so cool!" Lauren squealed. "Snow in Pasadena!" She picked up a chunk of snow and started rolling it up between her hands.

"Snowball fight!" she shouted.

"Stop it, Lauren!" I cried. "We're in big trouble here. Don't you understand—?"

Lauren fired the snowball at Nicole.

Instantly, thick white snow spread all over Nicole's body. Covering her. Covering her until she looked like a snowman!

"Nicole!" I cried, running over the snowy ground to her. "Nicole—are you okay?"

I grabbed her arm. Stiff as an icicle.

She was frozen solid!

226

"Nicole!" I stared into her snow-covered eyes. "Can you hear me, Nicole? Can you breathe in there? Nicole? Nicole?"

"Oh, no!" Lauren shrieked. "What have I done?"

My sister was a statue. A frozen, snow-covered statue.

"Nicole, I'm so sorry," Lauren cried. "Can you hear me? I'm so sorry!"

"Let's take her inside," I suggested frantically. "If we get her in the warm house, maybe we can warm her up."

Lauren grabbed one of Nicole's arms. I grabbed the other. We carefully dragged her stiff body to the house. Her bare toes, hard as ice, left a long trail in the snow.

"She's so freezing!" Lauren cried. "How can we melt the snow?"

"Let's put her next to the oven," I said. "Maybe if we turn it up full blast, the snow will melt."

We stood her in front of the oven. For good measure, I turned on all the burners on top of the stove.

"That ought to do it," I said. A bead of sweat

trickled down my face. From the heat—or from worry?

Lauren and I watched and waited.

Watched and waited.

I didn't move. I didn't breathe.

The snow didn't melt.

"It's not working," Lauren groaned. "Nothing's happening."

I tapped Nicole's arm. Solid ice.

I tried to stay calm. But I felt as if a hundred butterflies were tap-dancing in my stomach. "All right, it's not working. We'll have to try something else. Something else. . ."

Tears rolled down Lauren's cheeks. "Like what?" Lauren demanded in a trembling voice.

"Well. . ." I racked my brain for the hottest place I could think of. "The furnace! We'll hold her in front of the furnace."

We dragged Nicole into the furnace shed behind the garage. The snow seemed to weigh a ton. It took all our strength to drag her.

I turned the furnace on full blast. Lauren stood Nicole in front of the open furnace door.

A blast of hot air sent Lauren and me staggering back. "If this doesn't work, nothing will," Lauren sobbed.

The heat roared out of the furnace. I saw reflections of the red flames on Nicole's icy face.

My heart pounding, I watched to see the ice start to drip and the snow slide off her.

But the ice didn't melt. My sister remained a human snow cone.

"Jordan—what are we going to do?" Lauren wailed.

I shook my head, thinking hard. "The furnace isn't working. What else is hot?" I was too scared to think clearly.

"Don't worry, Nicole," Lauren told my frozen sister. "We'll get you out of this—somehow."

I suddenly remembered how warm the Abominable Snowman had felt when he carried us across the Alaskan tundra. There we were, ten degrees below zero, surrounded by deep snow, and heat had poured off the creature's body.

"Come on, Lauren," I ordered. "We're taking her to the darkroom."

Struggling and straining, we dragged Nicole back outside and across the back garden to the darkroom.

"Stay here," I told Lauren. "I'll be right back."

I raced into the kitchen. I pulled open all the cupboards and drawers, desperately searching for one thing—trail mix.

Please, please let there be trail mix somewhere in this house! I prayed.

"Yes!" I found a plastic bag of trail mix behind an old box of spaghetti. I grabbed it and flew back to the darkroom.

Lauren stared at the bag in my hand. "What's that?"

"Trail mix."

"Trail mix? Jordan, can't you wait to eat later?"

"It's not for me—it's for *him*." I motioned at the trunk.

"What?"

I unlatched the trunk and pulled it open. The Abominable Snowman lay inside as before, frozen in the block of ice.

I grabbed a handful of trail mix and waved it above the snowman's face. "Wake up!" I begged. "Please wake up! Look—I brought you some trail mix!"

"Jordan—have you totally lost it?" Lauren screeched. "What on earth are you doing?"

"I can't think of any other way to save Nicole!" I cried.

My hand trembled as I frantically waved the trail mix over the snowman. "Come on! You know you love trail mix. Wake up! Please wake up! Come out and help us."

I leaned over, staring hard at the monster's eyes. Watching for him to blink. Watching for any signs of life.

But the eyes didn't move. The creature stared lifelessly up through the block of ice.

I refused to give up.

"Yum, yum!" I shouted, my voice high and wild. "Trail mix! Boy, is that good!" I popped a few raisins into my mouth and chewed.

"Mmm-mm! Delicious trail mix. So good! So tasty! Come on—wake up and try some!"

"He's not moving!" Lauren sobbed. "Give up, Jordan. It isn't going to work."

I jumped when I heard a soft sound. A faint *crick*.

I stared down at the block of ice.

Did the monster move?

No. Silence now. The Abominable Snowman's black eyes glittered up at me, lifeless and blank.

Was it my imagination?

Lauren is right, I thought sadly. My plan isn't working.

Nothing is working.

I gently touched my sister's stiff, frozen arm. Maybe when Dad gets home, I hoped. Maybe he'll think of some way to save her.

"What are we going to *do*?" Lauren sobbed. She was no help at all.

Crack.

I heard it again—louder this time.

And then: *Crrraaaaaacccckkkk!*

A long crack ripped across the ice.

The Abominable Snowman groaned.

Lauren leaped back with a wild scream. "It's alive!"

The ice broke up. The furry snowman slowly pulled himself up, moaning.

Lauren cried out in fear. She pressed herself against the darkroom wall. "What's he going to do?"

"Shhh!"

The monster shook shards of broken ice from his shoulders. He lifted himself out of the trunk. He uttered a low growl.

"Jordan, look out!" Lauren cried.

The monster lurched towards me. My heart jumped. I wanted to back away—or *run* away. But I couldn't. I had to stay and help Nicole.

"Uh!" the snowman grunted. He swiped a giant paw at me.

Lauren let out another shrill scream.

I leaped back. What would the monster do?

"Uh!" the monster cried again. He took another swipe.

"Let's get out of here!" Lauren shouted. "He's going to hurt you!"

I wanted to run. But Nicole. . .

The monster swiped at me again—and snatched the bag of trail mix out of my hands.

I suddenly realized that was all he wanted. He had been grabbing for the trail mix.

He poured the trail mix into his mouth,

gulping it down, swallowing it noisily. Then he tossed the bag away.

Lauren pressed her back against the corner of the darkroom. "Make him go back into the trunk!" she cried.

"Are you crazy? How can I do that?"

The snowman growled and staggered across the floor.

His heavy footsteps shook the floor. He stopped in front of Nicole.

He reached his powerful arms around her snow-covered body—and squeezed.

"Stop him!" Lauren screamed. "He's crushing her!"

I couldn't move. I stared in horror.

The big creature hugged Nicole hard—so hard that he lifted her off the ground.

"Stop!" I finally choked out. "You're hurting her!"

Without thinking of the danger, I dived forward. I grabbed his furry arms with both hands—and struggled to pull him off my sister.

With an angry grunt, he brushed me away.

I stumbled back—and fell into Lauren.

I turned to see the monster squeezing Nicole.

Lauren pointed down at the floor. "Jordan— look!"

Gazing down, I saw a small puddle under Nicole's feet. Water dripped off her and on to the floor. As it hit the floor, it evaporated. Vanished from sight.

Did I see Nicole's toes wiggle?

Yes!

I stepped closer. Caught a glimpse of her face.

A dot of pink appeared on her cheeks.

Yes!

Chunks of snow dropped off her body. They thudded to the floor, melted, and disappeared.

I turned to Lauren. "It's working!" I cried happily. "He's defrosting her!"

A trembling smile crossed Lauren's worried face.

A few seconds later, the snowman let Nicole go. The ice and snow had all melted and disappeared. The snowman gave a satisfied grunt and stepped back.

Nicole moved her arms stiffly. She rubbed her face, as if she were waking up.

"Nicole!" I cried, grabbing her by the shoulders. Warm. Her shoulders were warm. "Are you okay?"

She shook her head, dazed. "What happened?"

Lauren ran up to Nicole and threw her arms around her. "You were frozen!" she said. "Frozen like a snowman! But thank goodness—you're all right!"

I turned to see the snowman watching us.

"Thank you," I called to him.

I don't know if he understood me. He grunted.

"Let's get out of here," Lauren urged. "I'm freezing!"

"Maybe the sun will warm you up," I told her.

We opened the darkroom door and stepped

237

outside. The sun still beamed down. The air felt sweltering hot. But the whole garden was covered in snow.

"Oh, yeah," Lauren murmured. "I forgot about that."

"Hey—!" I cried out when I saw the Abominable Snowman leap out of the darkroom. "He's escaping!" I shrieked.

"Dad will *kill* us!" Nicole cried.

All three of us started shouting at the creature.

He ignored our cries and thudded heavily across the snow. His black eyes narrowed on the snow-covered tree. He stepped up to the tree. Threw his arms around it. And hugged it tightly, just like when he had hugged Nicole.

I watched as the snow began to melt. The blanket of white slipped down, down, shrinking away—until the tree stood green and golden again under the sunlight.

"Wow!" I uttered, hands pressed against my face.

But the big, furry creature had more surprises in store.

With a loud grunt, he dropped to the snowy ground. As we stared in surprise, he began to roll in the snow.

The snow appeared to stick to his fur. As he rolled, the snow vanished beneath him.

Before long, the big creature was rolling on

green grass. The last of the snow had vanished.

He jumped to his feet. His eyes went wide, and he uttered a pained cry.

"What's the matter with him?" Lauren demanded.

The Abominable Snowman gazed around, stunned, at the green grass, the palm trees. Then he raised his eyes to the blazing sun.

He clutched his fur-covered head and let out a scream of terror.

He seemed confused for a moment. Frightened. Then he let out a deep grunt—and took off down the street. His big paws thudded heavily over the pavement.

I ran after him. "Wait! Come back!"

He tore through someone's garden and kept running.

I gave up. No way I could catch him.

Nicole and Lauren caught up with me. "Where's he going?" Nicole demanded.

"How should I know?" I snapped, struggling to catch my breath.

"I think he's looking for somewhere cold," Lauren said.

Nicole agreed. "You're probably right. He must be so hot. Pasadena is no place for an Abominable Snowman."

"He'll probably find a cave in the mountains," I said. "It's a lot colder up there. I only hope he finds a way to get trail mix."

We trudged back to our garden. Green again. And hot. I knew that Nicole and I had one word in our minds—D-A-D.

He had instructed us not to touch the trunk. We had ignored his warning.

Now the snowman was gone. Dad's big discovery. Dad's big chance for fame.

Gone. Gone for ever.

It was all our fault.

"At least Dad has his photos," I said softly. "The photos will amaze everyone all by themselves."

"I guess so," Nicole replied, biting her bottom lip tensely.

We walked back to the darkroom to close up the supply trunk. I glanced inside the trunk. Two magic snowballs were left.

"Those things are dangerous. We'd better get rid of them," Nicole warned.

"*I'm* not touching them." Lauren backed away.

"You're right," I told my sister. "We should hide them somewhere. They're too dangerous to keep around."

Nicole ran into the house and returned with a heavy-duty rubbish bag. "Quick—stuff them in here."

I carefully scooped up each snowball and dropped it in the trash bag. Then I twisted the bag closed and knotted it tightly.

"Now what?" Lauren asked.

"We should blast them into outer space," Nicole said. "If anyone gets hold of them and starts spreading snow around, we'll be in big trouble. We need the Abominable Snowman to get rid of the snow—and he's gone."

"Pasadena could turn into a ski resort!" I joked. "We could ice skate on Kyle and Kara's swimming pool."

I shivered. I didn't want to think about Kyle and Kara. And I didn't want to think about snow. "We should bury the snowballs," I told them. "But where?"

"Not in *my* garden!" Lauren protested.

I didn't want to bury them in our garden, either. What would happen to them down there? Would they spread snow underground? Would snow spring up through the grass?

We left the darkroom and scanned the area for good burial spots.

"What about the empty lot?" Nicole suggested.

Across the street, right next to Kyle and Kara Miller's house, stood a vacant lot. There was nothing in it but piles of sand and a few empty bottles.

"Perfect," I declared. "No one will ever find the snowballs there."

Nicole hurried to the garage and grabbed a shovel. We crossed the street, glancing around to make sure no one saw us.

"The coast is clear," I said.

I grabbed the shovel and dug a deep hole in the sand. It took longer than I thought. Sand kept falling back into the hole.

Finally, the hole was deep enough.

Nicole dropped the rubbish bag into the hole. "Goodbye, snowballs," she said. "Goodbye, Alaska."

I covered the hole with sand. Lauren smoothed it out so you couldn't tell the sand had been dug up.

"Phew," I groaned, wiping the sweat from my face. "I'm glad that's over. Let's go inside and cool off."

I put away the shovel. Then Nicole, Lauren and I got ourselves some cold apple juice and collapsed in front of the TV.

A short while later, we heard Dad's car pull into the driveway.

"Uh-oh," Lauren gasped. "I think I'd better go home now. See you guys later." She hurried out the back door. "Good luck!" she called. The door slammed behind her.

I gave Nicole a nervous glance. "How angry will Dad be? He finds an amazing, rare creature, brings it home—we let it loose, and it runs away. That's not so bad—*is* it?"

Nicole shuddered. "Maybe if we tell him the *whole* story, he'll be so glad we're not hurt that he won't be angry."

"Uh-huh. Yeah. Maybe."

The front door swung open. "Hey, kids!" Dad called. "I'm home! How's our snowman doing?"

We ate supper early that evening. Things were pretty quiet around the dinner table.

"I'm glad you kids are safe and sound," Dad said for the fifth time. "That's what counts."

"Yeah," Nicole said, chewing her pizza.

"Uh-huh," I added quietly. I usually had three slices. Tonight I could barely manage one. And I left the crust on the plate.

Poor Dad. He was trying so hard not to get upset about losing the Abominable Snowman. But Nicole and I knew how bad he felt.

Dad dropped his half-eaten slice of pizza on his plate. "I'll tell the Museum of Natural History that they'll have to make do with the photographs."

"Photographs are better than nothing," I said.

"Better than nothing? Are you crazy?" Nicole cried. "Those pictures are going to amaze the whole world!"

Dad perked up. "That's true. I mentioned

them to some TV producers. They went wild."

He stood and carried his plate to the sink. "I think I'll go out to the darkroom and develop that film right now. These pictures are going to cheer me up. I mean, they're historic. Historic!"

I was glad to see Dad snap out of his disappointment. Nicole and I followed him, eager to see the photos.

We sat quietly under the red light while Dad developed the negatives. At last he pulled the first set of contact sheets out of the chemical baths.

Nicole and I leaned close to see the pictures.

"Huh?" Dad uttered an astonished cry.

Snow. Nothing but snow. Ten pictures of snow.

"That's strange," Dad choked out. "I don't remember taking those shots."

Nicole flashed me an evil stare. I knew what she was thinking.

I held up my hands innocently. "I'm not playing any tricks. I swear!"

"You'd better not be, Jordan," Dad warned sternly. "I'm in no mood for kidding around."

Dad turned back to the chemical trays and developed another set of photos. As he pulled them up, dripping wet, we all squinted at them.

More snow. Nothing but snow.

"This can't be happening!" Dad screamed. "The Abominable Snowman—he should be standing right *there*!" He pointed.

His hands shook as he grabbed the rest of the negatives and held them up to the red light. "The tundra shots came out fine," he declared. "The dogs, the sled, the elk herd—all there. All perfect. All of them. But the shots in the monster's cave—"

His voice trailed off. He shook his head sadly. "I don't get it. I just don't get it. How could this be? Not a single shot of the creature. Not one."

I sighed. I felt so bad for Dad. I felt so bad for all three of us.

No Abominable Snowman. No photos of the Abominable Snowman.

It was almost as if he had never existed. As if the whole thing had never happened.

Nicole and I left Dad in the darkroom to finish his work.

We trudged around the house to the front. Nicole groaned and grabbed my arm. "Oh, no! Look!"

Across the street in the vacant lot, I saw the Miller twins kneeling down, digging in the sand.

"They're digging up the snowballs!" I gasped.

"Those creeps!" Nicole growled. "They must have been spying on us while we buried them."

"We've got to stop them!" I cried.

We hurried across the street, running full speed.

How I Got My
Shrunken Head

Have you ever played *Jungle King*? It's a computer game, and it's really cool. Unless you sink into a quicksand pit or get squeezed to death by the Living Vines.

You've got to be fast to swing from vine to vine without letting them curl around your body. And to grab the shrunken heads that are hidden under trees and bushes.

If you collect ten shrunken heads, you get an extra life. You need a *lot* of extra lives in this game. It's not for beginners.

My friends Eric and Joel play *Jungle King* with me. They are twelve, like me. My sister Jessica is eight. She hangs around, but we don't let her play. That's because she always dives into the quicksand pits. She likes the *thwuck thwuck thwuck* sound it makes when your body is being sucked under.

Jessica just doesn't get it.

"Mark, why can't we play a different game?" Joel asked me.

I knew why he wanted to stop. He had just been trampled by a red rhino, the meanest kind.

Joel, Eric and I were up in my room during our autumn half term break from school, huddled around my computer. Jessica was on the window seat, reading a book. Sunlight poured over her, making her red hair sparkle.

"Kah-lee-ah!" I shouted as I picked up my eighth shrunken head. *Kah-lee-ah* is my jungle cry. It's a word that popped into my head one day. I suppose I made it up.

My face was a few centimetres from the monitor screen. I ducked as spears came flying at me from behind a leafy fern.

"Kah-lee-ah!" I let out my battle cry as I picked up another shrunken head.

"Come on, Mark," Eric pleaded. "Don't you have any other games?"

"Yeah. Don't you have any sports games?" Joel demanded. "How about *March Madness Basketball*? That's a cool game!"

"How about *Mutant Football*?" Eric asked.

"I like *this* game," I replied, keeping my eyes on the screen.

Why do I like *Jungle King* so much? I think it's because I love swinging from vine to vine across the sky.

You see, I'm a little chubby. Actually, I'm

short and chubby. I'm built a bit like the red rhinos. And so I suppose I like being able to swing so lightly, to fly above the ground like a bird.

Also, it's an *awesome* game.

Joel and Eric don't like it because I always win. In our first game this afternoon, an alligator chewed Joel in half. I think that put him in a bad mood.

"Do you know what game my dad bought me?" Joel asked. "*Battle Solitaire*."

I leaned closer to the screen. I had to get past the biggest quicksand pit. One slip, and I'd be sucked into the sandy slime.

"What kind of game is that?" Eric asked Joel.

"It's a card game," Joel told him. "You know. Solitaire. Only the cards fight each other."

"Cool," Eric replied.

"Hey, guys—I'm in a tough spot here," I said. "Give me a break, okay? I've got to concentrate. I'm right over the quicksand pit."

"But we don't want to play any more," Eric complained.

I grabbed a vine. Swung hard. Then reached for the next one.

And someone bumped my shoulder. "Owww!"

I saw a flash of red hair and knew it was Jessica. She bumped me again and giggled.

I watched myself tumbling down on the screen. Sucked into the bottomless slime pit.

Thwuck thwuck thwuck. I died.

I spun around angrily. "Jessica—!"

"My turn!" She grinned at me, her wide, toothy grin.

"Now we have to start all over again!" I announced.

"No way," Eric protested. "I'm going home."

"Me, too," Joel said, pulling his baseball cap lower on his forehead.

"One more game!" I pleaded.

"Come on, Mark. Let's go outside," Joel said, pointing to the bright sunshine pouring through the bedroom window.

"Yeah. It's a great day out. Let's throw a Frisbee or something," Eric suggested. "Or get our skateboards."

"One more game. Then we'll go outside," I insisted.

I watched them head out of the door.

I really didn't want to leave the jungle. I don't know why I like jungles so much. But I've been really into jungles since I was a teeny kid.

I like to watch all the old jungle movies on TV. And when we were little, I used to pretend I was Tarzan, King of the Jungle. Jessica always wanted to play, too. So I let her be Cheetah, my talking chimpanzee.

She was very good at it.

But after she was six or seven, Jessica refused

to be a chimp any more. She became a full-time pest instead.

"I'll play *Jungle King* with you, Mark," she offered, after my two friends had left.

"No way," I replied, shaking my head. "You just want to take a dive into the quicksand pit."

"No. I'll play it right," she promised. "I'll try to win this time. Really."

I was about to let her play when the doorbell rang downstairs.

"Is Mum home?" I asked, listening for her footsteps.

"I think she's in the back garden," Jessica replied.

So I hurried downstairs to answer the front door. Maybe Eric and Joel had changed their minds, I thought. Maybe they've come back for another round of *Jungle King*.

I pulled open the front door.

And stared at the most disgusting thing I'd ever seen in my life.

I stared at a head.

A human head, wrinkled and leathery. About the size of a tennis ball.

The pale, dry lips were pulled back in a sneer. The neck was stitched closed with heavy black string. The eyes—solid black eyes—stared up at me.

A shrunken head. A real shrunken head.

I was so shocked, so totally *amazed* to find it at my front door, that it took me a long time to see the woman who was holding it.

She was a tall woman, about my mum's age, maybe a little older. She had short black hair with streaks of grey in it. She wore a long raincoat buttoned to the top even though it was a warm, sunny day.

She smiled at me. I couldn't see her eyes. They were hidden behind large black-framed sunglasses.

She held the shrunken head by the hair—

thick black hair. Her other hand held a small canvas suitcase.

"Are you Mark?" she asked. She had a soft, smooth voice, like someone in a TV commercial.

"Uh ... yeah," I replied, staring at the shrunken head. They never looked so *ugly* in photos I'd seen. So wrinkled and dry.

"I hope I didn't startle you with this thing," the woman said, smiling. "I was so eager to give it to you, I took it out of my bag."

"Uh ... *give* it to me?" I asked, not taking my eyes off it. The head stared back at me with those glassy black eyes. They looked more like teddy-bear eyes than human eyes.

"Your aunt Benna sent it for you," the woman said. "As a present."

She held out the head to me. But I didn't take it. I had spent all day collecting shrunken heads in the game. But I wasn't sure I wanted to touch this one.

"Mark—who is here?" My mum stepped up behind me. "Oh. Hello."

"Hello," the woman replied pleasantly. "Did Benna write and tell you I was coming? I'm Carolyn Hawlings. I work with her. On the island."

"Oh, my goodness," Mum exclaimed. "Benna's letter must have got lost. Come in. Come in." She pulled me back so that Carolyn could enter the house.

257

"Look what she brought for me, Mum," I said. I pointed to the small green head dangling by the hair from Carolyn's hand.

"Yuck!" Mum cried, raising a hand to her cheek. "That isn't real—*is* it?"

"Of course it's real!" I cried. "Aunt Benna wouldn't send a *fake*—would she?"

Carolyn stepped into the living room and set down her small suitcase. I took a deep breath. Worked up my courage. And reached for the shrunken head.

But before I could take it, Jessica swooped in—and grabbed it out of Carolyn's hand.

"Hey—!" I shouted, reaching for her.

She darted away, giggling, her red hair flying behind her. Holding the head in both hands.

But then she stopped.

Her smile faded. And she stared down at the head in horror.

"It bit me!" Jessica cried. "It *bit* me!"

I gasped. Mum squeezed my shoulder.

Jessica started to giggle.

One of her stupid jokes.

She tossed the head from hand to hand. And grinned at me. "You're stupid, Mark. You'll believe anything."

"Just give me back my head!" I cried angrily. I dived across the living room and grabbed for it.

She started to pull it away—but I held on tightly.

"Hey—you scratched it!" I shrieked.

She had. I held the head up close to my face to examine it. Jessica had scratched a long white line on the right earlobe.

"Jessica—please," Mum begged, crossing her arms and lowering her voice. That's what Mum does when she's about to get steamed up. "Behave. We have a guest."

Jessica crossed her arms and pouted back at Mum.

Mum turned to Carolyn. "How is my sister Benna doing?"

Carolyn pulled off her sunglasses and tucked them into a raincoat pocket. She had silvery grey eyes. She looked older without the dark glasses on. I could see hundreds of tiny wrinkles at the corners of her eyes.

"Benna is fine," she replied. "Working hard. Too hard. Sometimes she disappears into the jungle for days."

Carolyn sighed and started to unbutton her raincoat. "I'm sure you know Benna's work is her life," she continued. "She spends every minute exploring the jungles of Baladora. She wanted to come and visit. But she couldn't leave the island. So she sent me instead."

"Well, it's very nice to meet you, Carolyn," Mum said warmly. "I'm sorry we didn't know you were coming. But any friend of Benna's is more than welcome."

She took Carolyn's raincoat. Carolyn wore khaki trousers and a short-sleeved khaki shirt. It looked like a real jungle-exploring suit.

"Come and sit down," Mum told her. "What can I offer you?"

"A cup of coffee would be nice," Carolyn replied. She started to follow Mum to the kitchen. But she stopped and smiled at me. "Do you like your present?"

I gazed down at the wrinkled, leathery head in my hands. "It's beautiful!" I declared.

That night before going to bed, I placed the head on my dressing-table. I brushed its thick black hair straight back. The forehead was dark green and wrinkled like a prune. The glassy black eyes stared straight ahead.

Carolyn told me that the head was over one hundred years old. I leaned against the dressing-table and stared at it. It was so hard to believe that it had once belonged to a real person.

Yuck.

How had the guy lost his head? I wondered.

And who decided to shrink it? And who kept it after it was shrunk?

I wished Aunt Benna were here. She would explain everything to me.

Carolyn was sleeping in the guest room down the hall. We had sat in the living room, talking about Aunt Benna all night. Carolyn described the work Aunt Benna was doing on the jungle island. And the amazing things she was finding there on Baladora.

My aunt Benna is a very famous scientist. She has been on Baladora for nearly ten years. She studies the animals in the jungle. And the plant life, too.

I loved listening to Carolyn's stories. It was

as if my *Jungle King* computer game had come to life.

Jessica kept wanting to play with my shrunken head. But I wouldn't let her. She had already put a scratch on its ear.

"It's not a toy. It's a human head," I told my sister.

"I'll trade you two of my Koosh balls for it," Jessica offered.

Was she *crazy*?

Why would I trade a valuable treasure like this for two Koosh balls?

Sometimes I worried about Jessica.

At ten o'clock, Mum sent me up to my room. "Carolyn and I have some things to talk about," she announced. I said good night and made my way upstairs.

I placed the shrunken head on my dressing-table and changed into my pyjamas. The dark eyes in the head appeared to flash for a second when I turned out the lights.

I climbed into bed and pulled up the covers. Silvery moonlight washed into the room from the bedroom window. In the bright moonlight, I could see the head clearly, staring at me from the table-top, bathed in shadows.

What a horrible sneer on its face, I thought with a shiver. Why is it locked in such a fright-ening expression?

I answered my own question: You wouldn't

262

smile either, Mark, if someone shrunk your head!

I fell asleep staring at the ugly little head.

I slept heavily, without any dreams.

I don't know how long I slept. But sometime in the middle of the night, I was awakened by a terrifying whisper.

"Mark... Mark..."

"Mark... Mark..."

The eerie whisper grew louder.

I sat straight up, and my eyes shot open. And in the heavy darkness, I saw Jessica, standing beside the bed.

"Mark... Mark..." she whispered, tugging my pyjama sleeve.

I swallowed hard. My heart pounded. "Huh? You? What's your problem?"

"I-I had a bad dream," she stammered. "And I fell out of bed."

Jessica falls out of bed at least once a week. Mum says she's going to build a tall fence around Jessica's bed to keep her in. Or else buy her a king-size bed.

But I think Jessica would just roll around even harder in a big bed and still fall out. My sister is a pest even in her sleep!

"I need a drink of water," she whispered, still tugging my sleeve.

I groaned and pulled my arm away. "Well, go downstairs and get it. You're not a baby," I growled.

"I'm scared." She grabbed my hand and pulled. "You have to come with me."

"Jessica—!" I started to protest. But why bother? Whenever Jessica has a scary dream, I end up taking her downstairs for a glass of water.

I climbed out of bed and led the way to the door. We both stopped in front of the dressing-table. The shrunken head stared out at us in the darkness.

"I think that head gave me bad dreams," Jessica whispered softly.

"Don't blame the head," I replied, yawning. "You have bad dreams just about every night— remember? It's because you have a sick mind."

"Do not!" she cried angrily. She punched my shoulder. Hard.

"If you hit me, I won't get you a drink," I told her.

She reached out a finger and poked the shrunken head on one of its wrinkled cheeks. "Yuck. It feels like leather. It doesn't feel like skin."

"I guess heads get hard when you shrink them," I said, straightening the thick tuft of black hair.

"Why did Aunt Benna send you a shrunken head and not me?" Jessica asked.

I shrugged. "Beats me." We tiptoed out into the hall and turned towards the stairs. "Maybe it's because Aunt Benna doesn't remember you. The last time she visited us, you were just a baby. I was only four."

"Aunt Benna remembers me," Jessica replied. She loves to argue.

"Well, maybe she thinks that girls don't like shrunken heads," I said. We made our way down to the kitchen. The stairs squeaked under our bare feet.

"Girls like shrunken heads," Jessica argued. "I know I do. They're cool."

I filled a glass with water and handed it to her. She made gulping sounds as she drank. "You'll share your head with me—right?" she asked.

"No way," I told her.

How do you share a head?

We made our way back upstairs in the darkness. I took her to her room and tucked her in. Then I crept back to my room and slipped into bed.

I yawned and pulled the covers up to my chin.

I shut my eyes, but opened them again quickly. What was that yellow light across the room?

At first, I thought someone had turned the hall light on.

But, squinting across the room, I saw that it

wasn't a light. The head. The shrunken head—
it was glowing!

As if bright flames surrounded it. A shimmering yellow glow.

And in the glow, I saw the dark eyes gleam
and sparkle.

And then the lips—the thin, dry lips that had
been set in a hard scowl—the lips began to
twitch. And the mouth pulled up in a horrifying
smile.

"Nooooooo!"

I let out a terrified wail.

Glowing brightly, surrounded by eerie yellow light, the head grinned at me, its dark eyes flashing.

My hands thrashed at the covers. I struggled to pull myself out of bed. But my legs tangled in the blanket, and I fell with a hard *thud* to the floor.

"Nooooooo!" I cried. My body trembled so hard, I could barely scramble to my feet.

Gazing up, I saw the grinning head float over the dressing-table. Float into the air. Float towards me like a glowing comet.

No!

I covered my face to shield myself.

When I glanced back up, the shrunken head glowed on the table-top.

Had I imagined it floating up?

I didn't care. I ran out of the bedroom. "The

268

head! The head!" I shrieked. "It's glowing. The head is glowing!"

Jessica jumped out as I ran past her bedroom. "Mark—what's going on?" she called.

I didn't stop to answer. I kept on running, down the hall to Mum and Dad's room. "The head!" I wailed. "The head!" I was so terrified, I didn't know *what* I was doing!

The door was closed. But I shoved it open without knocking. Mum was lying on her back on her side of the bed. My dad was away this week on a business trip. But Mum still slept on her side of the bed.

As I burst in, she sat up and uttered a startled cry. "Mark?"

I ran up beside her. "Mum—the shrunken head—it started to glow!" I cried, my voice high and shrill. "It's glowing, and it—it *grinned* at me!"

Mum stood up and wrapped me in a hug. She felt so warm and soft. I was shaking all over. I suddenly felt as if I were a little boy again.

"Mark, you had a nightmare," Mum said softly. She ran her hand over the back of my hair, the way she used to do when I was little.

"But, Mum—"

"That's all it was. A nightmare. Take a deep breath. Look how you're shaking."

I pulled away from her. I knew it wasn't a

nightmare. I'd been wide awake. "Come and see," I insisted. "Hurry."

I pulled her out into the hall. A light clicked on in Carolyn's room, and her door swung open. "What's happening?" she asked sleepily. She was wearing a long black nightshirt.

"Mark says his shrunken head glowed," Mum reported. "I think he had a bad dream."

"No, I didn't!" I shouted angrily. "Come on. I'll show you!"

I started to pull Mum down the hall. But I stopped when I saw the intense expression on Carolyn's face. She had been sleepy a second ago. But now her eyes were wide, and she was staring at me hard. Staring at my face, studying me.

I turned away from her and nearly bumped into Jessica. "Why did you wake me up?" Jessica demanded.

I pushed past her and led everyone down the hall to my room. "The head glowed!" I cried. "And it smiled at me. Look. You'll see!"

I burst into my room and strode up to the dressing-table.

The head was gone.

I stared in shock at the bare table-top.

Behind me, someone clicked on the bedroom light. I blinked in the bright light, expecting the shrunken head to appear.

Where was it?

My eyes searched the floor. Had it fallen and rolled away? Had it floated out of the room?

'Mark—is this some kind of joke?" Mum asked. She suddenly sounded very tired.

"No—" I started. "Really, Mum. The head—"

And then I saw the sly grin on Jessica's face. And I saw that my sister had both hands behind her back.

"Jessica—what are you hiding?" I demanded.

Her grin grew wider. She never could keep a straight face. "Nothing," she lied.

"Let me see your hands," I said sharply.

"No way!" she replied. But she burst out laughing and brought her hands in front of her. And of course she had the shrunken head gripped tightly in her right hand.

271

"Jessica—!" I let out an angry cry and snatched it away from her. "It's not a toy," I scolded her angrily. "You keep your paws off it. You hear?"

"Well, it wasn't glowing," she sneered. "And it wasn't smiling, either. You made that all up, Mark."

"Did not!" I cried.

I examined the head. Its dry lips were pulled back into the toothless snarl it always had. The skin was green and leathery, not glowing at all.

"Mark, you had a bad dream," Mum insisted, covering her mouth as she yawned. "Put the head down, and let's all get some sleep."

"Okay, okay," I muttered. I flashed Jessica another angry look. Then I set the shrunken head down on the dressing-table.

Mum and Jessica walked out of my room. "Mark is such a jerk," I heard Jessica say, just loud enough for me to hear. "I asked him to share the shrunken head, and he said he wouldn't."

"We'll talk about it in the morning," Mum replied, yawning again.

I started to turn off the light. But I stopped when I saw Carolyn, still standing in the hall. Still staring hard at me, a really intense expression on her face.

She narrowed her silvery eyes at me. "Did you really see it glow, Mark?" she asked softly.

I glanced at the head. Dark and still. "Yeah. I did," I replied.

Carolyn nodded. She seemed to be thinking hard about something. "Good night," she murmured. Then she turned and padded silently back to the guest room.

The next morning, Mum and Carolyn greeted me with the biggest surprise of my life.

"Your aunt Benna wants you to go and visit her in the jungle," Mum announced at breakfast.

I dropped the spoon into my Honey Nut Loops. My mouth fell open to my knees. "Excuse me?"

Mum and Carolyn grinned at me. I guess they enjoyed shocking me. "That's why Carolyn came," Mum explained. "To take you back with her to Baladora."

"Wh-why didn't you *tell* me?" I shrieked.

"We didn't want to tell you until we worked out all the details," Mum replied. "Are you excited? You get to visit a real jungle!"

"Excited isn't the word!" I exclaimed. "I'm. . . I'm. . . I'm. . . *I don't know what I am!*"

They both laughed.

"I'm going too!" Jessica declared, bouncing into the kitchen.

I let out a groan.

"No, Jessica. You can't go this time," Mum

said, putting a hand on my sister's shoulder. "This is Mark's turn."

"That isn't fair!" Jessica wailed, shoving Mum's hand away.

"Yes, it is," I replied happily. "Kah-lee-ah!" I cheered. Then I leaped to my feet and did a celebration dance around the kitchen table.

"Not fair! Not fair!" Jessica chanted.

"Jessica, you don't *like* jungles," I reminded her.

"Yes, I do!" she insisted.

"Next time will be your turn," Carolyn said, taking a long sip of coffee. "I'm sure your aunt would love to show you the jungle, Jessica."

"Yeah. When you're older," I sneered. "You know, the jungle is too dangerous for a kid."

Of course, when I said that to my sister, I had no idea of just how dangerous the jungle could be. No idea that I was heading towards dangers I couldn't even imagine.

After breakfast, Mum helped me pack my suitcase. I wanted to bring shorts and T-shirts. I knew it was hot in the jungle.

But Carolyn insisted that I pack long-sleeved shirts and jeans, because of the scratchy weeds and vines we'd be walking through. And because of all the jungle insects.

"You have to protect yourself from the sun," Carolyn instructed. "Baladora is so close to the

275

equator. The sun is very strong. And the temperature stays in the nineties all day."

Of course I carefully packed the shrunken head. I didn't want Jessica to get her paws on it while I was away.

I know, I know. Sometimes I'm pretty mean to my sister.

As we drove to the airport, I thought about poor Jessica, staying home while I went off to exciting adventures with Aunt Benna.

I decided to bring her back a really cool souvenir from the jungle. Some poison ivy, maybe. Or some kind of poisonous snake. Ha-ha!

At the airport, Mum kept hugging me and telling me to be careful. Then she hugged me some more. It was really pretty embarrassing.

Finally, it was time for Carolyn and I to board the plane. I felt scared and excited and glad and worried—all at once!

"Be sure to send postcards!" Mum called as I followed Carolyn to the gate.

"If I can find a postbox!" I called back.

I didn't think they *had* postboxes in the jungle.

The flight was very long. So long, they showed three films in a row!

Carolyn spent a lot of time reading through her notebooks and papers. But when the flight attendants served dinner, she took a break. And she told me about the work Aunt Benna had been doing in the jungle.

Carolyn said that Aunt Benna had made many exciting discoveries. She had discovered two kinds of plants that no one had ever seen before. One is a kind of crawling vine that she named after herself. *Bennalepticus*. Or something like that.

Carolyn said that Aunt Benna was exploring parts of the jungle where no one had ever gone. And that she was turning up all kinds of jungle secrets. Secrets that will make Aunt Benna famous when she decides to announce them.

"When was the last time your aunt visited you?" Carolyn asked. She struggled to pull open the plastic wrapping around her cutlery.

"A long time ago," I told her. "I can hardly remember what Aunt Benna looks like. I was only four or five."

Carolyn nodded. "Did she give you any special presents?" she asked. She pulled out the plastic knife and started to spread butter on her dinner roll.

I scrunched up my face, thinking hard. "Special presents?"

"Did she bring you anything from the jungle when she visited you?" Carolyn asked. She lowered the dinner roll to the tray and turned to me.

She had her dark glasses on again, so I couldn't see her eyes. But I had the feeling she was staring at me, studying me.

"I don't remember," I replied. "I know she didn't bring me anything as cool as a shrunken head. That head is really awesome!"

Carolyn didn't smile. She turned back to her food tray. I could tell she was thinking hard about something.

I fell asleep after dinner. We flew all night and landed in South-east Asia.

We arrived after dawn. The sky outside the aeroplane window was a deep purple. A beautiful colour I'd never seen before. A big red sun rose slowly through the purple.

"We change planes here," Carolyn announced. "A huge jet like this could never land in Baladora. We have to take a tiny plane from here."

The plane was tiny, certainly. It looked like a toy. It was painted a dull red. It had two red propellers on the slender wings. I searched for the rubber bands that made the propellers spin!

Carolyn introduced me to the pilot. He was a young man in a red-and-yellow Hawaiian shirt and khaki shorts. He had slicked-back black hair and a black moustache. His name was Ernesto.

"Can this thing fly?" I asked him.

He grinned at me from beneath the moustache. "I hope so," he replied, chuckling.

He helped us up metal steps into the cabin. Then he hoisted himself into the cockpit. Carolyn and I filled the cabin. There was only room for the two of us back there!

When Ernesto started the engine, it chugged and sputtered like a power mower starting up.

The propellers began to twirl. The engine roared. So loud I couldn't hear what Ernesto was shouting to us.

Finally I figured out that he was telling us to fasten our seat-belts.

I swallowed hard and stared out of the tiny window. Ernesto reversed the plane out of the hangar. The roar was so loud, I wanted to cover my ears.

This is going to be exciting, I thought. It's sort of like flying inside a kite!

A few minutes later, we were in the air, flying low over the blue-green ocean. The bright morning sunlight made the water sparkle.

The plane bumped and jerked. I could feel the wind blowing it, making us bounce.

After a while, Carolyn pointed out the islands down below. They were mostly green, with ribbons of yellow sand around them.

"Those are all jungle islands," Carolyn told me. "See that one?" She pointed to a large,

279

egg-shaped island. "Some people found buried pirates' treasure on that island. Gold and jewels worth millions of dollars."

"Cool!" I exclaimed.

Ernesto leaned over the throttle and brought the plane lower. So low I could clearly make out trees and shrubs. The trees all seemed tangled together. I couldn't see any roads or paths.

The ocean water darkened to a deep green. The engine roared as the plane bounced against strong winds.

"That's Baladora up ahead!" Carolyn announced. She pointed out of the window as another island came into view. Baladora was larger than the other islands, and very jagged. It curved around like a crescent moon.

"I can't believe that Aunt Benna is down there somewhere!" I exclaimed.

Carolyn smiled beneath her dark glasses. "She's there, okay."

I glanced to the front as Ernesto turned in his seat to face us. I saw instantly that he had a troubled expression on his face.

"We have a little problem," he said, shouting over the roar of the engine.

"Problem?" Carolyn asked.

Ernesto nodded grimly. "Yes. A problem. You see . . . I don't know how to land this thing. You two will have to jump."

Panic made me gasp. "But—but—but—" I sputtered. "We don't have parachutes!"

Ernesto shrugged. "Try to land on something soft," he said.

My mouth dropped open. My breath caught in my chest. Both hands gripped the arms of the seat.

Then I saw the smile on Carolyn's face. She shook her head, her eyes on Ernesto. "Mark is too smart for you," she told him. "He's not going to fall for a dumb joke like that."

Ernesto laughed. He narrowed his dark eyes at me. "You believed me—right?"

"Ha-ha. No way!" I choked out. My knees were still shaking. "I knew you were kidding," I lied. "Sort of."

Carolyn and Ernesto both laughed. "You're mean," she told Ernesto.

Ernesto's eyes flashed. His smile faded. "You've got to get used to thinking fast in the jungle," he warned.

He turned back to the controls. I kept my eyes looking out of the window, watching the island of Baladora sweep beneath us. Broad-winged white birds swooped over the tangled green trees.

A short strip of land had been cleared near the south shore of the island. Beyond it, I could see ocean waves smacking against dark rocks.

The little plane hit hard as we landed—hard enough to make my knees bounce up in the air. We bounced again on the bumpy, dirt landing strip. Then we rolled to a stop.

Ernesto cut the engine. He pushed open the cabin door. Then he helped us out of the plane. We had to duck our heads.

Ernesto carried our suitcases out. Carolyn had her small canvas bag. My suitcase was a little larger. He set them down on the landing strip and gave us a quick salute. Then he climbed back into the little red plane and pulled the door closed behind him.

I shut my eyes as the propellers whirred, showering sand over me. A few seconds later, Ernesto took off. The plane nosed up steeply, just barely making it over the trees at the end of the landing strip.

The plane turned sharply and headed back over the water. Carolyn and I picked up our bags. "Where do we go now?" I asked, squinting in the bright sunlight.

Carolyn pointed. A clearing of tall grass stretched beyond the narrow, dirt airstrip. At the edge of the clearing where the trees started, I could see a row of low grey buildings.

"That's our headquarters," Carolyn told me. "We built the airstrip right next to it. The rest of the island is jungle. No roads. No other houses. Just wilderness."

"Do you get cable TV?" I asked.

She stopped short. Then laughed. I don't think she expected me to make a joke.

We carried our suitcases towards the low grey buildings. The morning sun was still low in the sky. But the air was already hot and wet. Hundreds of tiny white insects—some kind of gnat— hovered over the tall grass, darting one way then the other.

I heard shrill buzzing. And somewhere in the distance, the high cry of a bird, followed by a long, sad reply.

Carolyn walked quickly, taking long strides over the tall grass, ignoring the darting white gnats. I jogged to keep up with her.

Sweat ran down my forehead. The back of my neck started to itch.

Why was Carolyn in such a hurry?

"We're kind of trapped here, aren't we?" I said, studying the low, twisted trees, beyond the small headquarters buildings. "I mean, how do we get off the island when we're finished?"

"We radio for Ernesto," Carolyn replied, not

slowing her pace. "It takes him about an hour to get here from the mainland."

That made me feel a little better. I waded through the tall grass, struggling to keep up with Carolyn.

My suitcase began to feel heavy. I wiped sweat from my eyes with my free hand.

We were nearing the headquarters. I expected Aunt Benna to come running out to greet me. But I couldn't see any sign of anyone.

A radio antenna was perched off to the side. The low buildings were perfectly square. Flat-roofed. They looked like upside-down crates. Square windows had been cut in each wall.

"What is that stretched over all the windows?" I asked Carolyn.

"Mosquito netting," she replied. She turned back to me. "Have you ever seen a mosquito as big as your head?"

I laughed. "No."

"Well, you will."

I laughed again. She was joking—right?

We stepped up to the first building, the largest in the row. I set down my suitcase, pulled off my baseball cap, and mopped my forehead with my shirtsleeve. Wow. It was hot.

A screen door led into the building. Carolyn held it open for me.

"Aunt Benna—!" I cried eagerly. Leaving the

suitcase on the ground, I ran inside. "Aunt Benna?"

Sunlight filtered through the netting over the window. It took a few seconds for my eyes to adjust to the darker light.

I saw a table cluttered with test tubes and other equipment. I saw a bookshelf filled with notebooks and books.

"Aunt Benna?"

Then I saw her. Wearing a white lab coat. Standing with her back to me, at a sink against the wall.

She turned, wiping her hands on a towel.

No.

Not Aunt Benna.

A man. A white-haired man in a white lab coat.

His hair was thick and brushed straight back. Even in the dim light, I could see the pale blue of his eyes, blue as the sky. Such strange eyes. They looked like blue glass. Like marbles.

He smiled. Not at me.

He was smiling at Carolyn.

He motioned to me by tilting his head. "Does he have it?" he asked Carolyn. He had a scratchy, hoarse voice.

Carolyn nodded. "Yes. He has it." I could see that she was breathing hard. Short, shallow breaths.

Was she excited? Nervous?

A smile crossed the man's face. His blue eyes appeared to twinkle.

"Hi," I said awkwardly. I felt really confused. What did that question mean? What did I have?

"Where is my aunt Benna?" I asked.

Before he could answer, a girl appeared from the back room. She had straight blonde hair and the same pale blue eyes. She was dressed in a white T-shirt and white tennis shorts. She appeared to be about my age.

"This is my daughter Kareen," the man said in his hoarse voice, more like a whisper. "I am Dr Richard Hawlings." He turned to Kareen. "This is Benna's nephew. Mark."

"Tell me something I don't know," Kareen replied sharply, rolling her eyes. She turned to me. "Hey, Mark."

"Hi," I replied. Still confused.

Kareen flipped her blonde hair back over the shoulders of her T-shirt. "What grade are you in?"

"Sixth," I told her.

"Me, too. Except I'm not in school this term. I'm in *this* dump." She frowned at her father.

"Where is my aunt?" I asked Dr Hawlings. "Is she working or something? I thought she'd be here. You know. When I arrived."

Dr Hawlings stared at me with those strange blue eyes. It took him a long time to reply. Finally, he said, "Benna isn't here."

"Excuse me?" I wasn't sure I'd heard him correctly. It was hard to understand his raspy voice. "Is she . . . uh . . . working?"

"We don't know," he replied.

Kareen played with a strand of her hair. She twisted it around her finger, staring at me.

Carolyn stepped behind the lab table and leaned her elbows on it. She rested her head in her hands. "Your aunt Benna is missing," she said.

Her words made my head spin.

They were so unexpected. And she said them so flatly. Without any feeling at all.

"She's . . . *missing*?"

"She's been missing for a few weeks," Kareen said, glancing at her father. "The three of us—we've been trying really hard to find her."

"I-I don't understand," I stammered. I shoved my hands into my jeans pockets.

"Your aunt is lost in the jungle," Dr Hawlings explained.

"But—Carolyn said—" I started.

Dr Hawlings raised a hand to silence me. "Your aunt is lost in the jungle, Mark."

"But-but why didn't you tell my mum?" I asked, confused.

"We didn't want to worry her," Dr Hawlings replied. "Benna's your mum's sister, after all. So Carolyn brought you here because *you* can help us find her."

"Huh?" My mouth dropped open in shock. "Me? How can I help?"

Dr Hawlings stepped across the small room towards me. His eyes locked on mine. "You can help us, Mark," he said in his hoarse whisper. "You can help us find Benna—because you have Jungle Magic."

"I have *what*?"

I stared at Dr Hawlings. I didn't know what he was talking about.

Was *Jungle Magic* some kind of computer game? Was it like *Jungle King*?

Why did he think I had it?

"You have Jungle Magic," he repeated, staring back at me with those amazing blue eyes. "Let me explain."

"Daddy, give Mark a break," Kareen interrupted. "He's been flying for a hundred hours. He must be wrecked!"

I shrugged. "Yeah. I'm a little tired."

"Come and sit down," Carolyn said. She led me over to a tall stool beside the lab table. Then she turned to Kareen. "Do we have any Cokes left?"

Kareen pulled open a small fridge against the back wall. "A few," she replied, bending down to get to the bottom shelf. "Ernesto is supposed to bring another crate on his next flight."

Kareen brought me a can of Coke. I popped it open and tilted the can to my mouth. The cold liquid felt so good on my hot, dry throat.

Kareen leaned against the table, close to me. "Have you ever been to a jungle before?"

I swallowed more Coke. "No. Not really. But I've seen a lot of jungle movies."

Kareen laughed. "It's not like in the movies. I mean, there aren't herds of gazelles and elephants gathering at the water hole. At least, not on Baladora."

"What animals are on the island?" I asked.

"Mosquitoes, mostly," Kareen answered.

"There are some beautiful red birds," Carolyn said. "Called scarlet ibises. You won't believe their colour. A little like flamingos, only much brighter."

Dr Hawlings had been studying me the whole time. He walked over to the table and dropped down on to a stool across from me.

I held the cold Coke can against my hot forehead. Then I lowered it to the table. "Tell me about my aunt Benna," I said to him.

"Not much to tell," Dr Hawlings replied, frowning. "She was studying a new kind of tree snail. Somewhere on this end of the jungle. But one night she didn't return."

"We're very worried about her," Carolyn said, twisting a strand of hair. She bit her lower lip.

"Very worried. We searched and searched. Then we decided you could help us."

"But how can I help?" I demanded. "I told you—I've never been to a jungle."

"But you have Jungle Magic," Carolyn replied. "Benna gave it to you. The last time she visited you. We read about it. It's in Benna's notebooks over there."

Carolyn pointed to a stack of black notebooks on the bookshelf against the wall. I gazed at them, thinking hard. I still didn't understand.

"Aunt Benna gave me some kind of magic?" I asked.

Dr Hawlings nodded. "Yes, she did. She was afraid the secret might fall into the wrong hands. So she gave it to you."

"Don't you remember?" Carolyn asked.

"I was so little," I told them. "I was only four. I don't remember. I don't think she gave me anything."

"But she *did*," Carolyn insisted. "We know you have Jungle Magic. We know that you—"

"How?" I interrupted. "How do you know I have it?"

"Because you saw the shrunken head glow," Carolyn replied. "The head will only glow for people who have the magic. We read that in Benna's notebooks."

I swallowed hard. My throat suddenly felt dry again. My heart began to race.

"You're telling me I have some kind of special magic powers?" I asked in a tiny voice. "But I don't feel strange or anything. I've never done anything magic!"

"You have the magic," Dr Hawlings said softly. "The magic is hundreds of years old. It belonged to the Oloyan people. They used to live on this island."

"They were headshrinkers," Carolyn added. "Hundreds of years ago. That head I brought you—it was Oloyan. We have uncovered many others."

"But your aunt uncovered the secret of their ancient magic," Dr Hawlings said. "And she gave it to you."

"You've *got* to help us find her!" Kareen declared. "You've got to use the magic. We've got to find poor Benna—before it's too late."

"I'll try," I told them.

But secretly, I thought: they've made a big mistake.

Maybe they've mixed me up with someone else.

I don't have any Jungle Magic. None at all.

What am I going to do?

I spent the day exploring the edge of the jungle with Kareen. We uncovered some amazing yellow spiders that were nearly as big as my fist. And Kareen showed me a plant that can snap its leaves closed around an insect and keep it trapped for days until the plant has digested it all.

Pretty cool.

We climbed low, smooth-barked trees. We sat in the tree limbs and talked.

Kareen is okay, I think. She's very serious. She doesn't laugh a whole lot. And she doesn't like the jungle at all.

Kareen's mum died when she was a little kid. She wants to go back to New Jersey and live with her grandmother. But her father won't let her.

As I talked with her, I kept thinking about Jungle Magic. And I kept thinking about how—whatever it was—I didn't have it.

Sure, I always liked jungle movies. And jungle books and jungle games. I always thought jungles were really awesome. But that doesn't mean I have any special powers or anything.

And now Aunt Benna was missing. And her friends on Baladora were so desperate to find her, they had brought me here.

But what could I do?

What?

As I lay in bed that night, the question didn't go away.

I stared up at the low ceiling of the small wooden shack, wide awake. There were six or seven flat-roofed shacks in a row, behind the main building. We each had our own little shack to sleep in.

My little cabin had a narrow bed with a flat, lumpy mattress. A low bedside table where I placed my shrunken head. A small dressing-table with all the drawers stuck except the bottom one. A narrow wardrobe, just big enough for the clothes I'd brought. And a tiny bathroom in the back.

Through the netting over the open window, I could hear the chirp of insects. And in the distance, I heard a *caww caww caww*. Some sort of animal cry.

How can I help find Aunt Benna? I wondered as I stared up at the dark ceiling and listened to the strange sounds.

What can I do?

I tried to remember her. I tried to remember her visit to my house when I was four.

I pictured a short, dark-haired woman. Chubby like me. A round pink face. Intense dark eyes.

I remembered that she talked very quickly. She had sort of a chirpy voice, and she always seemed excited. Very enthusiastic.

And I remembered. . .

Nothing else.

That's all I could remember about my aunt.

Did she give me Jungle Magic? No. I didn't remember anything about that.

I mean, how do you give someone *magic*?

I kept thinking about it and thinking about it. I struggled to remember more about her visit.

But I couldn't.

I knew that Carolyn and Dr Hawlings had made a terrible mistake. I'll tell them in the morning, I decided. I'll tell them they got the wrong kid.

A terrible mistake . . . terrible mistake. The words repeated in my mind.

I sat up. I just couldn't get to sleep. My brain wouldn't let me. I was wide awake.

I decided to take a walk around the headquarters building. Maybe explore back where the trees grew thick and the jungle started.

I crept to the screen door and peered out. My

little cabin stood at the end of the row. I could see the other cabins from my door. All dark. Kareen, Carolyn and Dr Hawlings had gone to sleep.

Caww caww. The strange cry repeated in the distance. A soft wind made the tall grass bend and shift. Tree leaves rustled, making a whispering sound.

I was wearing a long, baggy T-shirt pulled down over boxers. No need to get dressed, I decided. No one else is awake. Besides, I'll just take a very short walk.

I slipped into my sandals. Pushed open the screen door. And stepped outside.

Caww caww. The cry sounded a little closer.

The night air felt hot and wet, nearly as hot as during the day. A heavy dew had fallen, and my sandals slid over the damp, tall grass. The wet grass tickled my feet through the sandals.

I made my way past the silent, dark shacks. To my right, the trees bent and swayed. Black shadows against a purple sky. No moon. No stars tonight.

Maybe taking a walk is a bad idea, I told myself. Maybe it's too dark.

I need a torch, I realized. I remembered Carolyn's warning earlier when she showed me where I would sleep. "Never go out at night without a torch. At night," she had warned me, "we are not in charge here. At night, this is the creatures' world."

The back of the headquarters building loomed ahead of me. I decided to turn round.

But before I could turn, I realized I wasn't alone.

In the darkness, I caught a pair of eyes, staring back at me.

I gasped. A chill ran down my back.

Staring hard through the purple night, I saw another pair of eyes.

And then another and another.

Dark eyes, staring at me without moving, without blinking.

Dark eyes, on top of each other.

I froze. I couldn't move.

I knew that I was trapped. There were too many of them. Too many.

My legs trembled. Chill after chill rolled down the back of my neck.

And as I stared at the eyes, the dark eyes in pairs, eyes on top of eyes—as I stared at them, they began to glow.

Brighter. Brighter.

And in the golden light, I saw that these were not creature eyes.

These were not animal eyes.

These were human eyes.

I was staring at the glowing eyes of a hundred shrunken heads!

A pile of shrunken heads. All heaped together. Eyes on top of eyes. Heads like tight fists, mouths curled into snarls, or open in toothless horror.

Heads on heads. Dark and wrinkled and leathery.

So terrifying in the cold golden glow from their eyes.

I uttered a choked cry—and took off.

My legs felt rubbery and weak. My heart pounded in my chest. I ran around the headquarters building, the yellow glow fading slowly from my eyes. I ran as fast as I could to the front of the dark building. To the screen door.

Gasping for breath, I pulled open the door. And leaped inside.

I pressed my back against the wall and waited. Waited for the eerie glow to fade completely. Waited for my heart to stop racing, for my breathing to slow.

After a minute or two, I began to feel a little calmer.

Those heads, I wondered. Why are they piled back there like that?"

I shook my head hard, trying to shake awake the ugly picture of them. They were all people once, I realized. Hundreds of years ago, they were people.

And now. . .

I swallowed hard. My throat felt tight and dry.

I started across the room to the fridge. I needed something cold to drink, I told myself. I bumped the edge of the lab table.

My hands shot out, and I knocked something over. I grabbed it before it rolled off the table.

A torch.

"Hey—!" I cried out happily.

I'm going to listen to Carolyn's advice from now on, I promised myself. I'm never going out again without a torch.

I pushed the button, and a white beam of light swept over the floor. As I raised the torch, the light settled on the bookshelf against the wall.

Aunt Benna's black notebooks flashed into view. A tall stack of them nearly filled the shelf.

I moved quickly to the bookshelf. With my free hand, I pulled down the top notebook. It was heavier than I thought, and I almost dropped it.

Cradling it in my arms, I carried it over to the lab table. I climbed on to the tall stool and opened it up.

Maybe I can find some answers in here, I thought.

Maybe I can find the part where Aunt Benna talks about giving me Jungle Magic. Maybe I can find out why Dr Hawlings and Carolyn think I have it.

I leaned over the notebook and aimed the light on to the pages. Then I began flipping through, page after page, squinting in the light.

Luckily, my aunt has big, bold handwriting. Very clear and easy to read.

The pages seemed to be organized by year. I kept flipping pages, scanning each page quickly—until I came to the year of her visit.

My eyes rolled down over a long section about

lizards. Some kind of tree lizards that Aunt Benna was studying.

Then she described a cave she had found, cut into the rocky shore at the other side of the island. The cave, she wrote, had been lived in by the Oloyans, maybe two hundred years ago.

I skimmed over long lists of things Aunt Benna had found in the cave. Her handwriting got very jagged, very crooked here. I guess she was really excited by her discovery.

I turned several more pages. And started a section marked "Summer".

As I read the words, my mouth dropped open. My eyes nearly bulged out of my head.

The words started to blur. I lowered the torch to the page so that I could see better. I blinked several times.

I didn't want to believe what I was reading.

I didn't want to believe what Aunt Benna had written.

But the words were there.

And they were terrifying.

The torch shook in my hand. I steadied it between both hands. Then I leaned forward and read Aunt Benna's words, moving my lips silently as I read.

"Dr Hawlings and his sister Carolyn will stop at nothing to destroy the jungle and all the creatures who live here," my aunt wrote in her bold, clear handwriting. "They do not care who they hurt or who they kill. They care only about getting what they want."

I swallowed hard. Steadied the circle of light over the notebook page. And kept reading.

"Finding the secret of Jungle Magic in that cave was my most amazing discovery," Aunt Benna wrote. "But I know the secret is not safe as long as Dr Hawlings and Carolyn are around. They will use the Jungle Magic to do evil. And so I have given the Jungle Magic and its secret to my nephew Mark. He lives four thousand miles away in the United States. And so I hope the secret will be safe.

"If the Jungle Magic ever falls into Hawlings's hands," my aunt continued, "the jungle will be destroyed. The island of Baladora will be destroyed. And so will I."

I gasped and turned the page. I struggled to keep the torch steady so that I could read more.

"If Hawlings gets the Jungle Magic," Aunt Benna wrote, "he will shrink my head until there is no trace of me. I must keep my nephew four thousand miles away from Hawlings. Because he will shrink Mark's head, too, to get at the magic I have hidden there."

"Ohhhh." A terrified moan escaped my throat.

Shrink my head?

Dr Hawlings will shrink my head?

I read the last words again: "I must keep my nephew four thousand miles away. . ."

But I'm *not* four thousand miles away! I told myself.

I'm here. I'm right here!

Carolyn brought me here to steal the magic. To take it from me. She and Dr Hawlings planned to shrink my head!

I slammed the notebook shut. I took a deep breath and held it. But it didn't help to slow the thudding of my heart.

What have they done to Aunt Benna? I wondered.

Did they try to get the secret from her? Did they do something terrible to her?

304

Or did she run away from them? Did she escape?

Did they bring me here to track her down so that they could capture her again? Then when I find her, do they plan to shrink *both* of our heads?

"Nooooo," I murmured, trying to stop my body from trembling.

I thought they were my friends. My friends. . .

But I'm not safe here, I told myself. I'm in terrible danger.

I have to get away. Get dressed and get away from these evil people. As fast as I can.

I dropped off the stool, turned, and started towards the door.

Got to get out. Got to get away.

The words repeated in rhythm with my pounding heart.

I reached for the screen door. Started to push it open.

But someone was standing there. Standing there in the deep shadows, blocking my escape.

"Where do you think you're going?" a voice called.

305

Kareen pulled open the door and stepped into the room. She wore an oversized T-shirt, down past her knees. Her blonde hair was dishevelled. "What are you doing in here?" she demanded.

"Let me go!" I cried. I raised the torch like a weapon.

She took a step back. "Hey—!" She let out a startled cry.

"I have to go," I insisted, pushing past her.

"Mark—what's your problem?" she asked. "Why are you acting so crazy?"

I stopped with the screen door half open, my shoulder against the frame. "I saw Aunt Benna's notebook," I told Kareen, shining the torch beam on her face. "I read what Aunt Benna said. About your father. And about Carolyn."

"Oh." Kareen let out a long sigh.

I kept the harsh light on her face. She

306

squinted at me, then covered her eyes with her arm. "Where is my aunt?" I demanded sharply. "Do you know where she is?"

"No," Kareen replied. "Lower the light—okay? You don't have to blind me."

I lowered the light. "Did your father do something terrible to my aunt? Did he hurt Aunt Benna?"

"No!" Kareen screamed. "How can you ask that, Mark? My father isn't evil. He and Benna just don't agree about some things."

"You're sure you don't know where my aunt is? Is she hiding somewhere? Hiding from your father? Is she still on the island?" The questions leaped out of me. I wanted to grab Kareen and force her to tell me the truth.

She tugged at both sides of her blonde hair. "We don't know where your aunt is. We really don't," she insisted. "That's why Carolyn brought you here. To help us find her. We're worried about Benna. We really are."

"That's a lie!" I cried angrily. "I read my aunt's notebook. Your father isn't worried about my aunt."

"Well, I am," Kareen insisted. "I like your aunt a lot. She's been really nice to me. I don't care about Daddy and Aunt Carolyn and their arguments with Benna. I'm worried about Benna. I really am."

I raised the torch again. I wanted to check out

307

Kareen's expression. I wanted to see if she was telling the truth.

Her blue eyes flashed in the light. I saw a teardrop running down one cheek. I decided she was being honest with me.

"Well, if you're worried about my aunt, help me get away from here," I said, lowering the light again.

"Okay, I'll help you," she answered quickly, without having to think about it.

I pushed open the screen door and crept outside. Kareen followed. She closed the door silently behind her. "Turn off the light," she whispered. "We don't want Daddy or Carolyn to see."

I clicked off the light and started over the wet grass towards my cabin, walking fast. Kareen hurried to keep at my side.

"I'll get dressed," I whispered. "Then I'm going to try to find Aunt Benna." A shudder swept down my back. "But how? Where should I go?"

"Use the Jungle Magic," Kareen whispered. "It'll tell you where Benna is. It'll tell you where to go."

"But I can't!" I cried shrilly. "Up until today, I didn't even know I *had* any kind of magic. I'm still not sure I believe it."

"Use the magic—" Kareen whispered, narrowing her eyes at me.

"But I don't know how!" I insisted.

"The magic will guide you," she replied. "I'm sure it will. I'm sure it will show you the way."

I wasn't so sure. But I didn't say anything.

My mind was spinning. Aunt Benna's written words kept weaving through my thoughts.

I should be four thousand miles away, I told myself. I'm only safe if I'm four thousand miles away.

Now, how will I escape from Carolyn and Dr Hawlings?

How?

We were striding down the row of cabins. The air still felt hot and wet, heavy. The sky had darkened to black. There were still no stars, no moon.

I'll get dressed, and I'll get away, I told myself.

Get dressed. Get away.

"Hurry, Mark," Kareen whispered at my side. "Hurry. And don't make a sound. Daddy is a very light sleeper."

My cabin came into view at the end of the row.

But before I could reach it, I heard the soft thud of footsteps on the grass. Rapid footsteps.

Kareen gasped and grabbed my arm. "Oh, no! It's *him*!"

I think I jumped a metre in the air.

Should I run? Try to hide?

If this was a game of *Jungle King*, I'd know the right moves. I'd know how to escape from the Evil Scientist. I'd grab a vine and swing myself to safety. And pick up a few extra lives along the way.

But, of course, this was no game.

I pressed my back against the cabin wall and froze there, waiting to be caught.

The rapid footsteps thudded closer.

I held my breath, but my heart still pounded.

I held my breath—and watched a funny-looking animal hop into view.

Not Dr Hawlings. But a weird-looking rabbit, with huge ears and big paws that thudded the ground as it hopped.

I watched the weird creature dart away, disappearing between two of the low cabins. "Is it a rabbit?"

Kareen raised a finger to her lips, reminding me to be quiet. "It's a new species of giant rabbit your aunt discovered."

"Very educational," I murmured. "But do I need a nature lesson now?"

Kareen pushed me by the shoulders towards my cabin door. "Hurry, Mark. If my dad wakes up. . ." She didn't finish her sentence.

If he wakes up, he'll shrink my head. I finished the sentence for her.

My legs suddenly felt as if they were about to collapse. But I forced myself into my dark cabin.

My hands were shaking so hard, I could barely get dressed. I pulled on the jeans I'd been wearing that day. And a long-sleeved T-shirt.

"Hurry!" Kareen whispered from the door. "Hurry up!"

I wished she'd stop saying that. I jumped every time.

"Hurry, Mark!"

I pulled open my suitcase and grabbed the torch I'd brought. Then I started to the door.

"Hurry, Mark. Get going!" Kareen whispered.

I stopped halfway across the cabin. Grabbed the shrunken head. Stuffed it into my T-shirt pocket. Then I pushed open the door and stepped back outside.

Where should I go? What should I do? How could I find my aunt?

A million questions rushed through my mind.

My throat felt so dry, it ached. I thought about getting one of those cold Cokes in the lab. But I knew I couldn't risk waking Kareen's father.

We started walking across the wet grass. "Don't turn on the torch until you're hidden by the trees," Kareen instructed.

"But where do I go? How do I find Aunt Benna?" I whispered, swallowing hard.

"There's only one path," Kareen told me, pointing to the tangled dark trees at the edge of the clearing. "It will lead you part of the way."

"Then what?" I demanded, my voice shaking.

Her eyes locked on mine. "The Jungle Magic will take you the rest of the way."

Yeah. Sure.

And next week, I'll flap my arms and fly to the moon.

I had the sudden urge to turn around. Go back to my little shack. Go to bed and pretend I'd never read my aunt's notebook.

But then Kareen and I passed the big pile of shrunken heads. The dark eyes all seemed to stare up at me. Such sad, sad eyes.

I don't want my head to end up on that pile, I decided. No way!

I started to jog towards the trees.

Kareen hurried to keep up with me. "Good luck, Mark!" she called softly.

"Th-thanks," I stammered. Then I stopped

312

and turned to her. "What are you going to tell your dad in the morning?"

Kareen shrugged. The wind blew her blonde hair around her face. "I won't tell him anything," she said. "I'll tell him I slept all night. That I didn't hear a thing."

"Thanks," I repeated. Then gripping the torch tightly, I turned and ran into the trees.

The path was soft and sandy. The sand felt wet through my sandals. Vines and big, flat leaves reached over the path. They slapped against my jeans legs as I trotted along.

Tall weeds grew over the path. After a minute or so, it became too dark to see. Had I wandered off the path?

I clicked on the torch and shone the light along the ground.

The light swept over the tall weeds, strange ferns, tendrils of vines. The black-trunked trees appeared to lean towards me, reaching for me with their smooth limbs.

No path.

Here I am, I thought, squinting into the pale beam of light. Here I am, all alone in the jungle.

Now what do I do?

"Ow!"

I swatted a mosquito on my neck. Too late. I could feel the throb of its bite.

Rubbing my neck, I took a few steps through the tall weeds. I kept the circle of light in front of my feet.

Aa-OO-tah. Aa-OO-tah.

A shrill cry—very close by—made me stop.

Night in the jungle belongs to the creatures, I remembered with a shiver.

Aa-OO-tah. Aa-OO-tah.

What *was* it?

Not a giant rabbit. But it sounded really BIG.

I spun the light in a circle, keeping it low over the grass and vines. The smooth tree trunks shone purple in the pale light.

I didn't see any animals.

I lowered the light.

My whole body was shaking. Despite the

damp heat of the night, I couldn't stop shivering.

A wind made the leaves all flap, the trees bend and whisper.

The jungle was *alive*, I realized.

Insects chittered all around. Fat leaves scraped and cracked. I heard the soft crackle of animal footsteps, running over the ground.

Aa-OO-tah. Aa-OO-tah.

What *was* that?

Without realizing it, I had pressed myself against a low tree. I took a deep breath and held it, listening hard.

Was the animal moving closer?

Thick clumps of leaves hung down from the low branches, forming a kind of cave. I'm protected under here, I thought, gazing all around. I suddenly felt a little safer, hidden under the thick leaves, under the low branches.

Through my leafy roof, I glimpsed a sliver of white moonlight. It made the leaves gleam like silver.

I clicked off the torch and lowered myself to a sitting position on the ground. Leaning back against the smooth trunk, I gazed up at the moon, taking slow, steady breaths.

As soon as I felt calmer, I realized how tired I was. The sleepiness swept over me like a heavy blanket. I yawned loudly. My eyelids seemed to weigh a tonne.

I tried to stay alert. But I couldn't fight the drowsiness.

With the chittering of insects for a lullaby, I leaned my head against the tree trunk and drifted into a deep sleep.

I dreamed about shrunken heads.

Dozens of shrunken heads, the leathery skin purple and green, the black eyes glowing like dark coals, the dry black lips pulled back in angry snarls.

The heads floated and danced through my dream. They darted back and forth like tennis balls. They flew into me, bounced against my chest, bounced off my head. But I didn't feel them.

They bounced and floated. And then the dry lips opened, and they all began to sing. "*Hurry, Mark. Hurry.*" That was their song.

The words came out hoarse and raspy. The sound of air rattling through dead leaves.

"*Hurry, Mark. Hurry.*" An ugly, frightening chant.

"*Hurry, Mark. Hurry.*"

The black lips twisted into a sneer as they sang. The coal eyes glowed. The heads—dozens of shrivelled, wrinkled heads—bobbed and bounced.

I woke up with the whispered words in my ear.

I blinked. Grey morning light shimmered

down through the tree leaves. My back ached. My clothes felt damp.

It took me a few seconds to remember where I was.

The frightening dream stayed in my mind. My hand slid up to my T-shirt pocket. I felt the shrunken head tucked tightly inside.

My face itched.

I reached up to scratch my cheek—and pulled something off it. A leaf?

No.

I squinted at the insect in my hand. A large red ant. Nearly the size of a grasshopper.

"Yuck!" I tossed it away.

My skin tingled. My back itched. Something moved up and down my legs.

I jerked myself up straight. Alert. Wide awake now.

Itching like crazy. My whole body tingling.

I stared down at myself. Stared down at my jeans and T-shirt.

And started to scream.

I jumped to my feet. I thrashed my arms in the air. I kicked my legs.

My body was covered with giant red ants.

Hundreds and hundreds of them. Crawling over my arms, my legs, my chest.

Their prickly legs scratched over my throat and the back of my neck. I pulled a fat one off my forehead. Then another off my cheek.

I reached up and felt them crawling in my hair.

"Ohhhh." A low moan escaped my throat as I slapped at my hair. Swept my hands through it. Watched the big red ants fall to the ground.

I felt them crawl over the backs of my hands. Hot and prickly. So big. And so many of them.

I dropped to my knees, slapping at my chest, pulling the insects off my neck. I began rolling frantically in the tall grass, dripping wet from the heavy morning dew.

I rolled and slapped at myself. Rolled over and

over, trying to flatten the insects, trying to kick them off me. I grabbed another handful out of my hair and heaved them into a leafy bush.

I struggled back to my feet, twisting and squirming. Pulling at the big red ants.

But there were too many of them. My skin itched and tingled. Their tiny feet prickled my arms, my legs, my chest.

It itched so badly, I felt I couldn't breathe.

I'm suffocating, I realized. The ants—they're going to *smother* me!

"Kah-lee-ah!" I screamed, squirming and slapping. "Kah-lee-ah!"

To my surprise, ants started to drop off my body.

"Kah-lee-ah!" I screamed again.

Ants showered down to the ground. They leaped out of my hair, dropped off my forehead, off the front of my shirt.

I stared in amazement as they fell to the ground. Then they scurried away, climbing over each other, stampeding over and under the tall grass.

I rubbed my neck. I scratched my legs. My whole body still tingled. I still itched all over.

But the big ants were gone. They had all jumped off when I shouted my special word.

Special word.

I glanced down over my shirt, trying to rub away the horrible tingling. Inside my pocket, the shrunken head's eyes glowed. A bright yellow glow.

"Whoa!" I grabbed the head and tugged it from the pocket. I held it up in front of me.

"Kah-lee-ah!" I shouted.

The eyes glowed brighter.

My special word.

Where did the word come from? I didn't know. I thought I'd made it up.

But I suddenly knew that the word was the secret behind the Jungle Magic.

The word—and the shrunken head.

Somehow the word brought the Jungle Magic to life. When I shouted it out, the ants jumped off me and hurried away.

I gazed at the glowing little head with new excitement. My heart pounded in my chest. I concentrated on the head, thinking hard.

I *did* have Jungle Magic.

Dr Hawlings and Carolyn were right.

I had Jungle Magic and didn't know it. And the word *Kah-lee-ah* was the key that unlocked it.

It had helped me get rid of those nasty red ants. Would it help lead me to Aunt Benna?

"Yes!" I cried out loud. "Yes!"

I knew that it would. I knew I could find her now.

I was no longer afraid of the jungle and its creatures. No longer afraid of anything that

320

might await me in this hot, tangled jungle.

I had Jungle Magic.

I had it—and I knew how to use it.

And now, I had to find Aunt Benna.

A red morning sun rose over the treetops. The air was already hot and damp. Birds chirped and twittered on the tree limbs above me.

Holding the torch in one hand and the shrunken head in the other, I started to run towards the sun.

I'm going east, I told myself. The sun comes up in the east.

Was it the right direction to find my aunt?

Yes. I was sure it was right. The Jungle Magic will lead me, I decided. I just need to follow it, and it will take me to Aunt Benna, wherever she is hiding on this island.

I ran over fat, leafy vines and low shrubs. I ducked under smooth white tree branches. Broad leaves of huge green ferns slapped at me as I ran through them.

The sun beamed down on my face as I made my way through a wide, sandy clearing. Sweat dripped down my forehead.

"Hey—!" I cried out as my feet slipped on the soft sand.

My feet slid. I lost my balance. My hands shot out. The torch and the shrunken head flew on to the sand.

"Hey—!"

I started to sink.

Sand rolled up over my ankles. Up my legs.

I kicked. I waved my arms wildly.

I pulled up my knees. Tried to step out of the deep sand.

But I was sinking, sinking faster now.

Sand up to my waist.

The more I struggled, the faster I sank.

Deeper, deeper. Down into the pit of sand.

17

I couldn't move my legs. I had sunk too deep in the hot, wet sand.

The sand crept up over my waist.

There's no bottom, I thought. I'm going to keep sinking. I'm going to sink down, down until it covers my head. Until I disappear for ever.

My friends Eric and Joel once told me that there is no such thing as quicksand. I wished they were here right now. I could show them how wrong they were!

I opened my mouth to shout for help. But I was too panicked to make a sound. Only a tiny squeak came out.

What good is shouting? I asked myself.

There's no one around for miles. No one who will hear me.

The sand felt thick and heavy as I slid down, down deeper into it. I stretched both hands up over my head, my hands grasping, as if trying to grab on to something.

I tried moving my legs. Tried to pump them, like treading water or pedalling a bike.

But the sand was too heavy. I was in too deep.

My chest heaved with terror now. I gasped in breath after breath.

I opened my mouth once again to call for help.

And had an idea.

"Kah-lee-ah!" I screamed, my voice high and frightened.

"Kah-lee-ah! Kah-lee-ah!"

Nothing happened.

"Kah-lee-ah! Kah-lee-ah!"

I screeched the word at the top of my lungs.

But I continued to sink deeper, deeper into the wet, marshy pit of sand.

"Kah-lee-ah!"

No. Nothing.

I waved my arms over my head. And stared up at the pale blue sky. At the trees at the edge of the clearing.

Nothing but trees as far as I could see.

No one around. No one to help me.

"Oh!" I suddenly realized why the magic word wasn't working. I didn't have the shrunken head. The head had flown from my hand when I fell into the sandpit.

Where was it? Where?

Did it sink into the sand?

My eyes frantically searched the yellow-brown surface. The wet sand bubbled all around me, making a *pock pock pock* sound. Like a thick soup.

I sank deeper.

And saw the shrunken head.

It lay on the surface. Its black eyes stared up at the sky. Its hair was tangled beneath it, spread over the sand.

With an excited cry, I stretched out both hands and tried to grab it.

No. Too far away. Just out of my reach. Centimetres out of my reach.

"Unnnnh." I uttered a low grunt as I struggled to grab it. Stretched out my hands. Stretched. Stretched.

I leaned forward into the sand. Leaned and stretched.

And grabbed for it. Grabbed for it, curling my fingers. Groaning and grunting. Reaching. Reaching across the wet sand.

But no.

I couldn't get it. The head lay so close to my fingertips.

So close, yet so far away.

No way. No way.

My fingers grabbed only air. I couldn't reach it.

I knew I was doomed.

My hands dropped heavily on to the wet sand. I let out a defeated sigh.

My hands made a loud slapping sound as they hit the sand.

And the head bounced.

"Huh?" I uttered a startled cry. My heart started to pound.

I slapped the surface of the wet sand again with both palms.

The head bounced. Closer.

Another hard slap. Another bounce.

The head lay only a couple of centimetres away now.

I grabbed it, held it tightly—and joyfully shouted out the word. "*Kah-lee-ah! Kah-lee-ah!*"

At first, nothing happened.

My breath caught in my throat. I froze.

"*Kah-lee-ah! Kah-lee-ah!*"

I expected to fly up. To be lifted out of the sandpit. To float magically over to hard ground.

"Jungle Magic—please work! Please work!" I cried out loud.

But I didn't move. I sank a little deeper. The sand crept up over my chest.

I stared at the shrunken head in my hand. The black eyes appeared to stare back at me.

"Help me!" I cried. "Why aren't you helping me?"

And then I saw the vines.

Yellow-green vines creeping over the sandpit. Moving like long snakes. A dozen twisting, crawling vines, slithering towards me from all directions.

My heart pounded as I watched the vines slither closer. Closer. Until I reached out with my free hand and grabbed for the end of one.

But the vine swept past my hand, moving quickly with surprising force. It wrapped itself around my chest—and started to tighten.

"No!" I uttered a cry of protest. Was it going to strangle me?

Another vine dipped into the sand. I felt it curl around my waist.

"No—stop!" I wailed.

The vines tightened around me. And then they began to pull.

The wet sand made a *thwock* sound as I started to move through it.

Holding the shrunken head in the air, I let the vines tug me through the sand. They pulled hard and fast. The sand flew at my sides.

A few seconds later, the vines tugged me, on

my knees, on to hard ground. I let out a happy cry. The vines instantly let go. I watched them pull back, curling quickly into the tall weeds.

I hunched there, struggling to catch my breath, watching until the vines slithered out of sight. Then I pulled myself to my feet.

My legs felt shaky and weak. My whole body trembled from my close call.

But I didn't care. I felt like jumping up and clapping and shouting for joy. The Jungle Magic had worked. The Jungle Magic had saved me once again!

The wet sand clung to my jeans, my shirt, my arms—even my hair! I shook myself furiously. I tucked the shrunken head into my shirt pocket. Then I began slapping at my clothes, brushing off chunks of sand.

Now what? I asked myself, glancing quickly around. The sun had risen high in the sky. The trees and ferns and tall grass gleamed, a shimmering blur of green and gold. The air had grown hot. My shirt clung wetly to my back.

Now what?

How do I find Aunt Benna?

I pulled the shrunken head from my pocket and held it in front of me. "Lead the way," I ordered it.

Nothing happened.

I brushed chunks of sand off its leathery skin. I pried sand from between its thin black lips.

I turned towards the sun and took a few steps. Was I still walking east?

To my surprise, the dark eyes on the shrunken head suddenly started to glow.

What did that mean? Did that mean I was getting close to Aunt Benna? Did it mean I was walking in the right direction?

I decided to test it.

I spun around and started walking back towards the sandpit.

The eyes on the head instantly dimmed back to black.

I turned and started walking north.

The eyes remained dark.

I turned back in the direction of the sun.

Yes! The eyes began to glow again. "Kah-lee-ah!" I cried happily. The head was guiding me to my aunt.

Animals howled and insects chittered loudly as I made my way through the trees and tall weeds. It all sounded like music to me now.

"Aunt Benna, here I come!" I cheered.

I found myself walking deeper into the jungle. I had to keep ducking my head to avoid low branches and thick vines that stretched from tree to tree.

I heard weird bird calls overhead. As if the birds were talking to each other. As I ducked under a low limb, the whole tree seemed to shake. And a thousand black birds leaped off the branches, cawing angrily, so many of them they darkened the sky as they flapped away.

I suddenly came to a small clearing that forked into two branches, one to the left, one to the right. Which way should I go?

I held the shrunken head in front of me, watching it carefully. I started to the left.

The eyes grew dark. Wrong way.

I turned and started to the right, watching the eyes begin to glow again.

Was Aunt Benna hiding somewhere in these trees? Was I getting close?

The trees ended suddenly again, and I found myself in a grassy clearing. I squinted in the bright sunlight, my eyes sweeping over the shimmering green grass.

A low growl made me spin back towards the trees.

"Oh—!" I let out a sharp cry as I saw the tiger. My legs nearly crumpled under me.

The tiger raised its head in another growl. An angry growl. It pulled back its lips, baring enormous teeth. It arched its back, its yellow-brown fur standing straight on end.

Then with a furious hiss, it came charging at me.

The tiger's huge paws pounded over the grass. Its yellow eyes burned into mine.

I glimpsed two little cubs behind it, nestled in the shade of a tree.

"I'm not going to hurt your cubs!" I wanted to cry.

But of course there was no time.

The tiger let out a furious roar as it charged.

The roar drowned out my cry as I raised the shrunken head in front of me in a trembling hand. "Kah-lee-ah!"

My voice came out in a whimper.

I nearly dropped the head. My knees collapsed. I sank to the grass.

The tiger closed in for the kill. Its heavy paws thudded the dirt as it leaped towards me.

The ground felt as if it were shaking.

The ground *was* shaking.

To my horror, I heard a deafening *ripping*

332

sound. Like Velcro being torn apart. Only a thousand times louder.

I let out a cry as the ground trembled. Shook. Split apart.

The grass tore away. The dirt split in two. The earth opened up.

And I started to fall. Down into an endless hole in the earth.

Down, down.

Screaming all the way.

"Owww!"

I landed hard on my elbows and knees. Pain shot through my body. I actually saw stars! Hundreds of them, all red and yellow.

Trying to blink them away, I raised myself to my knees.

The shrunken head had bounced out of my hand. I spotted it a metre or so away in the dirt. I dived for it, grabbed it up in my shaking hand, and held on to it tightly.

I felt dizzy and shaken. I closed my eyes and waited for the dizziness to pass.

When I opened them, I realized I had fallen into a deep pit. Walls of dirt surrounded me. The blue sky was a small square high above my head.

Jungle Magic had saved me once again. The magic had caused the ground to split open so that I could fall to safety. So that I could escape the tiger.

I heard a low growl above me.

With a frightened cry, I gazed up to the top of the pit. And saw two yellow eyes glaring down at me.

The tiger snarled, baring its teeth.

I didn't escape, I realized.

I'm trapped down here. If the tiger leaps down into the pit, it will finish me off in seconds.

I have nowhere to run. No way to escape.

I fell back against the wall of dirt. I stared up at the snarling tiger. It eyed me hungrily, roaring again. Preparing to leap to the attack.

"Kah-lee-ah!" I cried. "Kah-lee-ah!"

The tiger roared in reply.

I pressed my back against the dirt. Tried to stop my whole body from shaking.

Please don't come down here! I begged silently. *Please don't jump down into this pit!*

The yellow eyes glowed in the sunlight. The silver whiskers twitched as the tiger snarled its toothy warning.

And then I saw a little yellow-and-black cat face appear at the top of the pit. One of the tiger cubs. It peered down at me over the edge of the grass.

The other cub popped up beside it. It leaned over the pit edge. Leaned so far, it nearly fell in!

The tiger moved quickly. She lowered her head—and bumped the cub away from the edge.

Then she picked up the other cub in her teeth and carried it away.

I swallowed hard. I didn't move. My back pressed against the cool dirt, I stared up to the top. Watched the square of blue sky. And waited for the tiger to return.

Waited.

And waited. Holding my breath.

Silence now. So silent I could hear the wind rushing through the tall grass.

A chunk of dirt broke off the pit wall and toppled to the bottom, crumbling as it landed. I kept my gaze on the opening, listening hard, watching for the tiger.

After what seemed like hours, I let out a long whoosh of air. I stepped away from the dirt wall and stretched.

The tiger isn't coming back, I decided.

She only wanted to protect her cubs from me. By now, she has taken them away. Far away.

I stretched again. My heart was still thumping hard in my chest. But I was starting to feel a little more normal.

How do I get out of here? I wondered, gazing at the steep dirt walls. Can I climb out?

I tucked the shrunken head back into my pocket. Then I dug both hands into the soft, cool dirt and tried to climb.

I pulled myself up about a metre. But then the dirt broke off under my trainers. It crumbled and fell, sending me sliding back to the bottom.

No. No way. I can't climb out, I realized.

I reached for the shrunken head. I'll have to use Jungle Magic, I decided.

The magic got me down here. Now I can use it to get me out.

I raised the head in front of me. But before I could call out the word, darkness fell over the pit.

Is the sun setting already? I wondered.

I gazed up to the top.

No. It wasn't evening. The square of sky that I could see was still bright blue.

Someone stood up there, blocking the sunlight.

The tiger?

A human?

I squinted hard, struggling to see.

"Who-who's there?" I called.

A face leaned over the edge, peering down at me. Squinting into the bright sunlight, I saw straight blonde hair. Pale blue eyes.

"Kareen!" I shouted.

She cupped her hands around her mouth. "Mark—what are you doing down there?"

"What are *you* doing here?" I cried.

Her hair fell over her face. She brushed it back. "I—I followed you. I was so worried about you!"

"Get me out of here!" I shouted up to her. I tried climbing again. But the dirt slid out from under my trainers.

"How?" she called down.

"I guess you didn't bring a ladder with you?" I shouted.

"Uh—no, Mark," Kareen sniped.

I guess she doesn't have much of a sense of humour.

"Maybe I could drop a rope down or something," she suggested.

"Rope isn't too easy to find in the middle of the jungle," I reminded her.

She shook her head. Her face tightened into a fretful frown.

"How about a vine?" I called up. "See if you can find a long vine. I could climb up a vine."

Her expression brightened. She disappeared. I waited impatiently. And waited. "Please hurry," I murmured out loud, my eyes on the square opening at the top. "Please hurry."

I heard the squawk of birds somewhere up above. Fluttering wings. More squawking and cawing.

Are the birds frightened? I wondered. If they are, *why*? Has the tiger returned?

I pressed against the dirt wall, watching the sky.

Finally, Kareen reappeared. "I found a vine. But I don't know if it's long enough."

"Lower it over the side," I instructed her. "Quick. I have to get out of here. I feel like a trapped animal."

"It was hard to pull it out of the ground," she complained. She began lowering the vine. It looked like a long snake twining down the side of the pit.

It stopped a metre above my head. "I'm going to jump up and grab it," I told Kareen. "Then I'll try to climb while you pull. Wrap the other end around your waist, okay? Just don't let go of it!"

"Just don't pull me down with you!" she called back.

I waited for her to tie the vine around herself. Then I bent my knees and jumped. I missed the end of the vine by a centimetre.

This was one of those times I wished I were tall and thin instead of short and chubby.

But I grabbed the vine on my third try. I wrapped both hands around it.

Then I pressed the soles of my trainers against the dirt wall. And started to pull myself up, like a mountain climber.

The dirt kept crumbling out from under me. And the vine grew more and more slippery as my hands started to sweat. But with Kareen cheering me on, I scrambled to the top.

I lay in the tall grass for a moment, breathing in the sweet fragrance. It felt so wonderful to be out of that deep hole.

"How did you fall down there anyway?" Kareen asked, tossing her end of the vine to the ground.

"It was easy," I replied. I climbed to my feet and tried to brush the dirt off my clothes.

"But didn't you see that big pit there?" she demanded.

"Not exactly," I told her. I wanted to change

the subject. "How did you find me? What are you doing here, Kareen?"

Her blue eyes locked on mine. "I was worried about you. I—I didn't think you should be all alone in the jungle. So I sneaked away. Daddy was working in his lab. I crept away from the headquarters, and I followed you."

I brushed clumps of dirt from my hair. "Well, I'm glad," I confessed. "But aren't you going to be in major trouble with your dad and Carolyn?"

She bit her lower lip. "Probably. But it will be worth the risk—if we find your aunt."

Aunt Benna!

Trying to survive the quicksand and the tiger, I had nearly forgotten about her.

A shadow rolled over us. The air suddenly grew cooler. I glanced up at the sky. The sun was lowering itself behind the trees.

"It's almost night," I said quietly. "I—I hope we can find Aunt Benna before it gets really dark."

I had already spent one night out in the jungle. I didn't want to spend another.

"Do you know which way to go?" Kareen asked. "Are you just wandering around, hoping to get lucky?"

"No way," I replied. I pulled the head from my shirt pocket. "This little guy is showing me the way."

"Excuse me?" Kareen's face filled with surprise.

"The eyes light up when I go the right direction," I explained. "At least, I *think* that's why they light up."

Kareen gasped. "You mean, you really *do* have Jungle Magic?"

I nodded. "Yeah. I have it. It's so weird. There's a word I've always said. 'Kah-lee-ah'. Just a crazy word. I thought I'd made it up when I was a little kid. But it's the word that makes the Jungle Magic work."

"Wow!" Kareen exclaimed. A grin spread across her face. "That's *awesome*, Mark! That means we really will find Benna. That's so great!"

The shadows over the ground grew longer as the sun dipped lower. I shivered as a cool gust of wind blew over us.

My stomach growled. I couldn't remember when my last meal was. I tried not to think about food. I had to keep moving.

"Let's get going," I said softly. I raised the head in front of me. Then I turned slowly—one direction, then the next—until the eyes began to glow. "This way!" I cried, pointing across the clearing to the trees.

We started walking side by side. The tall grass swished, brushing our legs as we stepped through it. Insects chittered in the trees.

Kareen stared in amazement at the glowing eyes on the leathery head. "Do you really think it's guiding us to Benna?"

"We'll soon find out," I said solemnly.

We stepped into the shifting darkness beneath the tangled trees.

As the sunlight faded, the jungle sounds changed. The birds in the trees stopped chirping. The shrill sawing of the insects grew louder. We heard strange animal howls and cries in the distance, the sound bouncing between the smooth trees.

I hoped the howls and cries *stayed* in the distance!

Dark creatures slithered through the tall weeds and low, fat ferns and shrubs. The shrubs appeared to tremble as night creatures scurried through them.

I heard the warning hiss of snakes. The eerie hoot of an owl. The soft flap of bat wings.

I moved closer to Kareen as we walked. The sounds were all so much more realistic than in my *Jungle King* game!

I'll probably never play that game again after this, I thought. It will seem far too tame.

We pushed our way through a clump of tall,

344

stiff reeds. The eyes on the shrunken head dimmed to black.

"Wrong way!" I whispered.

Kareen and I turned until the eyes glowed again. Then we moved forward, making our own path. We stepped over thick vines and pushed through tangles of weeds and low shrubs.

"Ow!" Kareen slapped at her forehead. "Stupid mosquito."

The shrill scratching of insects grew louder, drowning out the crunch of our trainers over the leaves and vines on the jungle floor.

As the darkness deepened, the eyes on the shrunken head appeared to glow brighter. Like twin torches, guiding us through the trees.

"I'm getting kind of tired," Kareen complained. She ducked her head to avoid a low branch. "I hope your aunt is nearby. I don't know how much longer I can walk."

"I hope she's nearby, too," I murmured in reply. I'd had a pretty exhausting day myself.

As we walked, I couldn't help thinking about Aunt Benna and her notebook. I didn't want to make Kareen feel bad. But I had to say something.

"My aunt didn't write very nice things about your dad and Carolyn in her notebook," I said, keeping my eyes at my feet. "I was kind of surprised."

Kareen was silent for a long moment. "That's

so horrible," she said finally. "They worked together for so long. I know they had an argument."

"About what?" I asked.

Kareen let out a sigh. "Daddy has some plans to develop the jungle. He thinks there are valuable minerals here. Benna thinks the jungle should be preserved."

She sighed again. "I think that's what they fought about. But I'm not sure."

"The notebook made it seem like your dad is evil or something," I muttered, avoiding her eyes.

"Evil? Daddy?" she cried. "No. No way. He's very strong-minded. That's all. He isn't evil. And I know that Daddy still cares about Benna. He still respects her and cares about her. He's really worried about her. He—"

"Whoa." I grabbed Kareen's arm, interrupting her. "Look." I pointed through the trees.

I spotted a clearing up ahead. And against the grey sky, I could see the black outline of a small shack.

Kareen gasped. "That little house. Do you think—?"

We both crept to the edge of the clearing. Something scurried quickly over my trainers, but I ignored it.

My eyes were on the tiny, dark shack.

As we moved closer, I could see that it was

346

built of tree limbs and sticks. Clumps of fat leaves made the roof. It had no window. But there were narrow openings between the branches.

"Hey—!" I whispered. I saw a pale light flicker in one of the openings.

A torch? A candle?

"Someone is in there," Kareen whispered, narrowing her eyes at the shack.

I heard a cough.

A woman's cough? Aunt Benna's cough? I couldn't tell.

"Do you think it's my aunt?" I whispered, huddling close to Kareen.

"Only one way to find out," she whispered back.

The shrunken head glowed brightly in my hand. The eerie yellow-green light splashed over the ground as Kareen and I crept closer.

Closer.

"Aunt Benna?" I called in a tiny voice. I cleared my throat. My heart pounded. "Aunt Benna? Is that you?"

I called again and stepped close to the open doorway of the small shack. I heard a thump inside. Saw a flash of light. And heard a startled cry.

A lantern appeared in the doorway. My eyes went to the pale yellow light. And then moved up to see the woman holding the lantern.

She was short—very short. Only about a foot taller than me, and a little chubby. Her straight black hair was tied back. In the glow of lantern light, I saw that she wore khaki slacks and a khaki safari jacket.

"Who's there?" She raised the lantern in front of her.

"Aunt Benna?" I cried, moving closer. "Is that you?"

"Mark? I don't believe it!" she exclaimed. She came running towards me, the lantern swinging at her side. The light bounced over the tall grass, making shadows dance.

She wrapped me in a hug. "Mark—how did

you find me? What are you doing here?" She had a high, chirpy voice, and she talked rapidly, without taking a breath.

She pushed me away from her to study my face. "I don't believe I even recognized you. I haven't seen you since you were four!"

"Aunt Benna—what are you doing out here?" I demanded breathlessly. "Everyone is so worried—"

"How did you get to Baladora?" she asked, gripping my shoulder with her free hand, holding the lantern high with the other. "What are you doing in the jungle? How did you get here?" she cried again.

"I—I used the Jungle Magic," I stammered.

Her eyes went wide. With surprise? With fear?

I suddenly realized she wasn't looking at me. "Hello. Who are you?" Aunt Benna asked quietly, stretching the lantern towards the trees.

Kareen stepped out from the edge of the clearing. In all the excitement, I didn't realize that she had lingered behind.

"That's Kareen," I told my aunt. "Do you know Kareen? Dr Hawlings's daughter?"

Aunt Benna gasped. She squeezed my shoulder. "Why did you bring her here? Don't you realize—?"

"It's okay," Kareen said quickly. "I was

worried about you. That's why I followed Mark."

"She helped me," I explained to Aunt Benna. "Kareen helped me get away from them. From Dr Hawlings and Carolyn. Kareen helped me get through the jungle."

"But—but—" Aunt Benna sputtered. "You told her about the Jungle Magic?"

"I only came to help!" Kareen insisted. "My father is worried about you. He—"

"Your father wants to *kill* me!" Aunt Benna cried angrily. "That's why I had to run away. That's why I had to leave everything behind and hide in the jungle." She glared at Kareen, her eyes squinting, her face pinched and hard in the yellow lantern light.

"Kareen is okay," I assured her. "She only wants to help, Aunt Benna. Really."

My aunt turned to me. "Carolyn and Hawlings brought you here?"

I nodded. "Yes. To find you. Carolyn brought me this." I pulled the shrunken head from my shirt pocket. It had stopped glowing.

"They told me I had Jungle Magic," I continued. "I didn't know what they meant. I thought they were crazy. Then, when I went out to look for you in the jungle, I discovered that I *did* have it."

Aunt Benna nodded. "Yes. You have it, Mark. I gave it to you when I visited you. When you were four. I hypnotized you. And I transferred the Jungle Magic from me to you. To keep it safe."

"Yes. I read your notebook," I told her. "I read about why you gave me the magic. But it didn't say what Jungle Magic is. I only know—"

"It's a powerful force," my aunt replied, lowering her voice. "It's a powerful force that will do your will, carry out your wishes."

Her eyes filled with sadness. "But we cannot talk about it now," she said in a whisper. "We are in danger here, Mark. Real danger."

I started to reply. But I heard rustling, cracking sounds from the trees. Footsteps?

All three of us spun round towards the sound.

To my surprise, Kareen started running across the grass. She cupped her hands around her mouth. "Over here, Daddy!" she shouted. "Over here! I found Benna, Daddy! Hurry!"

25

I gasped in shock.

No time to run.

A beam of light flickered out from the trees. Behind it came Dr Hawlings, trotting over the tall grass. He carried a torch in one hand. The light swept into my eyes, then moved over Aunt Benna.

Was Dr Hawlings carrying a gun? Some kind of weapon? I couldn't see. And I didn't want to find out.

I grabbed Aunt Benna's arm and tugged. I wanted to run, to escape into the jungle.

But my aunt refused to move. She seemed frozen in surprise. Or fear.

Kareen's father trotted up to us, breathing hard. Even in the dim light, I could see the pleased smile on his face.

"Good work, Kareen." He patted her shoulder. "I knew that if you helped Mark escape, he would lead us right to his aunt."

Still holding on to Aunt Benna's arm, I stared at Kareen angrily. She had tricked me. She had pretended to be my friend. But the whole time, she was working to help her father.

Kareen stared back at me for a moment. Then she lowered her eyes to the ground.

"Why did you trick me?" I demanded. "Why did you do it, Kareen?"

She raised her eyes to me. "Daddy needs the Jungle Magic," she replied softly.

"But you *lied* to me!" I cried.

"I didn't have a choice," Kareen said. "If your father needed your help, what would *you* do?"

"You did the right thing, Kareen," Dr Hawlings told her.

He raised the light to Aunt Benna's face. He forced her to cover her eyes. "Did you really think you could hide for ever, Benna?" he demanded softly.

"I—I'm sorry," I told my aunt. "It's my fault. I—"

"No." Aunt Benna put a hand on my shoulder. "It's not your fault, Mark. It's my fault. You didn't know anything about any of this. And now I'm afraid I've got you into a lot of trouble."

Dr Hawlings sniggered. "A lot of trouble. That's the truth." He stepped up to Aunt Benna. "I want the secret of Jungle Magic. Tell me the secret, Benna. Let me know how it works. And

353

I will allow you and your nephew to leave the island in one piece."

In one piece?

I didn't like the sound of that.

As Dr Hawlings stared at my aunt, I slipped the shrunken head from my pocket. I'll use the Jungle Magic, I decided. I'll use the magic to get us out of this jam.

I raised the head slowly in front of me. I opened my mouth to call out the secret word.

But I was stopped when I caught Aunt Benna's glance.

She was signalling to me with her eyes. Telling me not to do it.

"What's going on?" Dr Hawlings demanded, angrily turning to me. "What are you doing?"

"Don't give it away, Mark," Aunt Benna pleaded. "Don't let them know the secret word."

I lowered the shrunken head. "I won't," I whispered.

"It's okay, Daddy," Kareen said, her eyes on me. "I know the word. Mark told it to me. I can tell you what it is. It's—"

I clamped my hand over Kareen's mouth. "Run!" I cried to Aunt Benna. "Run—now!"

With an angry cry of attack, Aunt Benna lowered her shoulder and barrelled into Dr Hawlings. She roared into him like a football player—and sent him sprawling against the little shack.

He uttered a startled yelp. The torch flew out of his hand and rolled across the ground.

I spun away from Kareen and followed my aunt. Our shoes thudded over the tall grass as we ran for the trees.

We were nearly to the edge of the clearing when Carolyn stepped in front of us. "What's your hurry?" she demanded, moving to block our way. "The party is just starting."

Aunt Benna and I whirled around. Dr Hawlings had moved up behind us. We were trapped.

Carolyn raised her torch. Her silvery eyes narrowed at Aunt Benna. Carolyn smiled. A cold, unpleasant smile. "How are you, Benna? We missed you."

"Enough chitchat," Dr Hawlings muttered, gesturing with his torch. "It's too dark to go back to the headquarters. We'll have to spend the night here."

"How cosy," Carolyn said, still smiling that cold smile at Aunt Benna.

Aunt Benna scowled and looked away. "Carolyn, I thought you were my friend."

"We're all good friends here," Dr Hawlings said. "And good friends like to share. That's why you're going to share the secret of Jungle Magic with us, Benna."

"Never!" my aunt declared, crossing her arms in front of her.

"*Never* isn't a word for friends," Dr Hawlings scolded. "In the morning, we will go back to the headquarters. Then you will share everything, Benna. You will share all of your secrets. And you will give the Jungle Magic to Carolyn and me."

"Like a good friend," Carolyn added.

"Let's go," Dr Hawlings said. He put a heavy hand on my back and shoved me towards the little shack. Kareen was sitting on the ground, her collar pulled up, her back leaning against one wall.

"You and Benna—in the shack," Dr Hawlings ordered, giving me another rough shove. "That way, we can keep an eye on you."

"You're wasting your time, Richard," Aunt Benna told him. She was trying to sound tough, but her voice trembled as she said it.

Dr Hawlings forced us into the dark shack. Aunt Benna and I stretched out on the floor. Through the cracks in the wall, I could see the darting light of their torches.

"Are they going to guard us all night?" I whispered.

Aunt Benna nodded. "We're their prisoners now," she whispered back. She sighed. "But we can't let them have the Jungle Magic. We can't!"

I slid closer to my aunt. "If we don't give it to them," I said softly, "what will they do to us?"

Aunt Benna didn't reply.

"What will they do to us?" I repeated.

She stared down at the floor and didn't answer.

A red ball of a sun was rising in the early morning sky when Dr Hawlings poked his head into the shack and woke us up.

I had slept only a few minutes. The shack had no floor, and the ground was hard.

Whenever I closed my eyes, I dreamed about the shrunken head in my pocket. I dreamed that I held it to my hand. It blinked its eyes and its lips began to move.

"You are doomed!" it exclaimed in a horrifying, hoarse whisper. *"You are doomed. Doomed. Doomed!"*

Aunt Benna and I scrambled out of the shack, stretching and yawning. Even though the sun was still low over the trees, the air already felt hot and wet.

My whole body ached from lying on the hard ground. My shirt was damp and smelly. My stomach growled. I scratched my neck and discovered it was covered with mosquito bites.

Not one of the best mornings.

And it wasn't going to get any better.

We walked for hours through the sweltering jungle. Carolyn and Kareen led the way. Dr Hawlings walked behind Aunt Benna and me, making sure we didn't try to escape.

No one said a word. The only sounds were the cries of animals, the chirping of birds overhead, and the swish of the tall weeds and grass as we pushed through.

Swarms of white gnats flew up off the path, swirling together like small tornadoes. The sun beamed down through the trees, burning the back of my neck.

When we finally made it back to the row of cabins, I was hot, sweaty, starving and dying of thirst.

Dr Hawlings shoved Aunt Benna and me into an empty cabin. He slammed the door behind us and locked it.

The cabin had two folding chairs and a small bed without sheets or blankets. I dropped down wearily on to the bare mattress. "What is he going to do to us?"

Aunt Benna bit her lip. "Don't worry," she said softly. "I'll figure something out." She crossed the small room and tried the window. It was either stuck or bolted from the outside.

"Maybe we can break the glass," I suggested.

"No, he'll hear it," Aunt Benna replied.

I rubbed the back of my neck. The mosquito bites were itching like crazy. I wiped sweat off my forehead with the back of my hand.

The door opened. Kareen entered, carrying two small bottles of water. She tossed one to me and one to my aunt. Then she turned quickly, closed the door hard behind her, and carefully locked it.

I tilted the bottle to my mouth and gulped down the water without taking a breath. There were a few drops left at the bottom. I sprinkled them over the top of my head. Then I tossed the bottle to the floor.

"What are we going to do?" I asked Aunt Benna.

She was sitting in one of the folding chairs, her feet resting on the other. She raised a finger to her lips. "Ssshhh."

Outside, I heard the rattle of machinery. A metallic clang. I heard the rush of water from a hose.

I hurried to the window and peered out. But it faced the wrong way. I couldn't see anything.

"We've had one lucky break," Aunt Benna murmured.

I stared at her. "Excuse me?"

"One lucky break," she repeated. "Hawlings didn't take away the shrunken head. It was so dark last night, I don't think he saw it."

I pulled the head out from my pocket. The black hair had become tangled. I started to smooth it back.

"Put it away, Mark," Aunt Benna ordered sharply. "We don't want Hawlings to see it. He doesn't know that the head is needed for Jungle Magic."

"This particular head?" I asked, shoving it back in the pocket. "Only this head?"

Aunt Benna nodded. "Yes. That head and the magic word. The word I gave you when I hypnotized you. When you were four."

The head's black hair fell over my pocket. I carefully tucked it inside.

Outside, I heard another metallic clank. I heard a splash. The roar of water grew louder.

"We are in terrible danger," Aunt Benna said softly. "You will have to use the Jungle Magic to save us, Mark."

I felt a chill of fear. But I muttered, "No problem."

"Wait till I give you the signal," Aunt Benna instructed. "When I blink my eyes three times, pull the shrunken head out and shout the word. Keep watching me. Watch for the signal—okay?"

Before I could reply, the door burst open. Dr Hawlings and Carolyn hurried in, their faces grim.

Dr Hawlings carried a large silvery pistol.

"Outside," he ordered, waving the pistol at Aunt Benna and me.

Carolyn led the way down the row of cabins. She turned and made us stop behind the main headquarters building. Kareen stood against the wall, a wide-brimmed straw hat pulled down over her eyes.

The sun beamed down. The back of my neck prickled and itched.

Huddling close to my aunt, I squinted into the bright sunlight. To my right, the big pile of shrunken heads came into focus.

The dark eyes on the leathery, purple-and-brown heads seemed to stare at me. The mouths were all twisted in ugly expressions of anger and horror.

I turned away from the terrifying pile of tiny heads—to see something even more terrifying.

An enormous black pot stood behind the headquarters building. Water brimmed over the top, bubbling and boiling.

The pot stood on some kind of electric burner. Like a stove burner. It glared red hot. The boiling water inside the pot bubbled and steamed.

I turned to Aunt Benna and caught the fear on her face. "You can't do this!" she screamed to Dr Hawlings. "You know you can't get away with this!"

"I don't want to hurt you," Dr Hawlings said

362

calmly, without any emotion at all. A smile spread over his face. "I don't want to harm you, Benna. I just want to own the Jungle Magic."

I kept my eyes locked on my aunt. Waiting for her signal. Waiting for the three blinks that meant I should go into action.

"Give me the Jungle Magic," Dr Hawlings insisted.

Carolyn stepped up beside him, hands on her waist. "Give it to us, Benna. We don't want trouble. We really don't."

"No!" The word shot out of my aunt's mouth. "No! No! No! You both know that I will never give up the secret of Jungle Magic. Not to you. Not ever!"

Carolyn sighed. "Please, Benna. Don't make it difficult."

My aunt stared back at her. "Never," she murmured.

Aunt Benna blinked.

I swallowed hard, watching for two more blinks.

No. Not the signal. Not yet.

Dr Hawlings stepped forward. "Please, Benna. I'm giving you one last chance. Tell us the secret—now."

Aunt Benna shook her head.

"Then I have no choice," Dr Hawlings said, shaking his head. "Since you two are the only ones in the world who know the secret, you are both too dangerous. The secret must die with you."

"Wh-what are you going to do to us?" I blurted out.

"We're going to shrink your heads," Dr Hawlings replied.

The pot hissed as water boiled over the side. I stared in horror at the billows of steam rising up over the pot.

Was he really going to shrink our heads?

Was I going to end up shrivelled and leathery, with a head the size of a doorknob?

I forced my legs to stop wobbling and stared at Aunt Benna. Stared at her. Stared hard. Watching her eyes. Waiting for the three blinks.

Hurry! I pleaded silently. *Hurry—before he tosses us into the boiling water!*

Kareen watched in silence. What was she thinking? I wondered. I couldn't see her expression. Her face was hidden under the brim of the straw hat.

"Benna, one last chance," Dr Hawlings said softly. "Because I like you. And I like your nephew. Don't let me harm your nephew, Benna. Do it for him, okay? Tell me the secret— for Mark's sake."

"It isn't worth it, Benna," Carolyn chimed in. "It will be so easy for you to give the Jungle Magic to us."

"I—I can't," Aunt Benna stammered.

"Then we have no choice," Dr Hawlings said, almost sadly. "The boy goes in first."

He took a step towards me.

Aunt Benna blinked. Once. Twice. Three times.

Finally!

With a trembling hand, I tugged the head from my pocket.

I raised it in front of me. I opened my mouth to shout the secret word.

But Dr Hawlings swiped the head from my hand.

He grabbed it from me—and tossed it on to the big pile of heads.

Then he dived for me, reaching out to grab me with both hands.

I ducked out from under him.

And threw myself on to the disgusting pile of heads.

I began frantically sorting through them with both hands. Picking one up, tossing it aside. Grabbing the next one. The next one. The next one.

They felt sticky and warm. Hard as baseballs. The hair brushed my hands. The dark eyes stared up at me blankly. They were so ugly, my

366

stomach tightened. My breath came in wheezing gasps.

Behind me, I could hear my aunt struggling with Dr Hawlings. Wrestling with him. Trying to keep him away from me.

I heard Carolyn's shouts. Kareen's cries of alarm.

I had to find *my* shrunken head.

I had to find it before Dr Hawlings broke free of my aunt and grabbed me.

I picked one up. Tossed it down. Picked up another. Tossed it down.

How could I find mine?

Which one was it?

Which one? Which one?

I grabbed a head. Saw ants crawling over its cheeks.

Picked up another.

It stared at me with glassy green eyes.

Picked up another.

It had a long white scratch on its ear.

I started to toss it back on to the pile.

But stopped.

A white scratch on its ear?

Yes! Mine had a scratch! My sister Jessica— she had scratched it back home!

Yes! This head was mine!

"Thank you, Jessica!" I cried at the top of my lungs.

With an angry cry, Dr Hawlings dived at me. He wrapped his arms around me and started to drag me off the pile of heads.

"Kah-lee-ah!" I shouted, holding on tightly to the shrunken head. *My* shrunken head. "Kah-lee-ah!"

368

Will it save Aunt Benna and me? I wondered.

Will the Jungle Magic work this time?

Dr Hawlings still had his arms around my shoulders. He was still trying to pull me towards the boiling pot.

"Kah-lee-ah!" I screamed.

His hands slid away.

They seemed to shrink. His arms seemed to shrink into his body.

"Huh?" I uttered a startled cry when I realized that *he* was shrinking. Dr Hawlings's entire body was shrinking, growing smaller and smaller!

I raised my eyes to Kareen and Carolyn. They were shrinking, too. Shrinking down to the ground.

Kareen disappeared under the straw hat. Then she came running out from under the brim. A tiny Kareen, about the size of a mouse.

All three of them—Kareen, Carolyn, and Dr Hawlings—scampered over the grass. Mouse-sized. Squeaking angrily in tiny mouse voices.

I stood beside the pile of heads and watched them scurry over the ground. Squeaking and squealing. I watched them until they disappeared into the jungle.

Then I turned back to Aunt Benna. "It worked!" I cried. "The Jungle Magic—it saved us!"

She rushed forward and wrapped me in a hug.

"You did it, Mark. You did it! The jungle is safe now! The whole world is safe!"

There were more hugs when Aunt Benna flew me home. Hugs from Mum—and even Jessica.

They met us at the airport. Then Mum drove us home for a big welcome-home dinner. I had so many stories to tell, I started telling them in the car. And I didn't stop talking until way past dinner.

It was nearly bedtime when Aunt Benna led me into the living room. She closed the door behind us. Then she sat me down on the sofa.

She sat down beside me. "Look into my eyes," she said softly. "Look deeply, Mark. Very deeply."

I raised my eyes to hers. "What are you going to do?" I asked.

I didn't hear her reply.

As I stared into her eyes, the room grew fuzzy. The colours all seemed to shift and blur. I thought I saw the posters on the living room wall flipping over and over. I thought I saw the chairs and coffee table sliding across the floor.

After a while, the room came back into focus. Aunt Benna smiled at me. "There," she said, squeezing my hand. "You're back to normal, Mark."

"Huh?" I squinted at her. "What do you mean?"

"No more Jungle Magic," she explained. "I took it back. You're a normal boy again."

"You mean, if I shout 'Kah-lee-ah' nothing will happen?" I asked.

"That's right." She smiled at me, still holding my hand. "I took back the magic. The shrunken head has no powers. And you have no powers. You never have to worry about it again."

She stood up, yawning. "It's getting late. Bedtime, don't you think?"

I nodded. "Yeah. I guess." I was still thinking about how I didn't have Jungle Magic any more. "Aunt Benna?"

"Yes?"

"Can I keep the shrunken head?"

"Of course," she replied, tugging me to my feet. "Keep the shrunken head. As a souvenir. That way, you will always remember your jungle adventure."

"I don't think I could forget it too easily," I replied. Then I said good night and made my way to bed.

The next morning, I woke up early and pulled on my clothes as fast as I could. I couldn't wait to get to school and show off the shrunken head to Eric and Joel and all the other kids.

I gulped down my cornflakes and orange juice. I strapped on my rucksack. Said goodbye to

Mum. Grabbed the shrunken head and headed out of the door.

Holding the head carefully in my hand, I started to jog along the pavement. It was a bright, sunny day. The air smelled warm and sweet.

My school is only three blocks from my house. But as I jogged along, it seemed like miles.

I couldn't wait to get there and show off to everyone.

I couldn't wait to tell my friends about all my jungle adventures.

I could see the school in the next block. And I could see a bunch of kids hanging out by the front door.

As I ran across the street, I suddenly felt the head move in my hand.

It twitched.

"Huh?" I let out a gasp and stared down at it.

The eyes blinked, then stared up at me. The lips closed, then opened again. "Hey, kid," the head growled. "Let *me* tell the part about the tiger!"

Reader beware – here's THREE TIMES the scare!

Look out for these bumper GOOSEBUMPS editions. With three spine-tingling stories by R.L. Stine in each book, get ready for three times the thrill … three times the scare … three times the GOOSEBUMPS!

Reader beware – you choose the scare!

A scary new series from R.L. Stine – where
you decide what happens!

Choose from over 20 scary endings!

HIPPO GHOST

Secrets from the past... Danger in the present...
Hippo Ghost brings you the spookiest of tales...

Castle of Ghosts
Carol Barton
Abbie's *bound* to see some ghosts at the castle where
her aunt works – isn't she?

The Face on the Wall
Carol Barton
Jeremy knows he must solve the mystery of the face on
the wall – however much it frightens him...

Summer Visitors
Carol Barton
Emma thinks she's in for a really boring summer, until she
meets the Carstairs family on the beach. But there's
something very *strange* about her new friends...

Ghostly Music
Richard Brown
Beth loves her piano lessons. So why have they started to
make her *ill*...?

A Patchwork of Ghosts
Angela Bull
Who is the evil-looking ghost tormenting Lizzie, and why
does he want to hurt her...?

The Ghosts who Waited
Dennis Hamley
Everything's changed since Rosy and her family moved
house. Why has everyone suddenly turned against her...?

The Railway Phantoms
Dennis Hamley
Rachel has visions. She dreams of two children in strange,
disintegrating clothes. And it seems as if they are trying
to contact her. . .

The Haunting of Gull Cottage
Tessa Krailing
Unless Kezzie and James can find what really happened in
Gull Cottage that terrible night many years ago, the
haunting may never stop. . .

The Hidden Tomb
Jenny Oldfield
Can Kate unlock the mystery of the curse on Middleton
Hall, before it destroys the Mason family. . . ?

The House at the End of Ferry Road
Martin Oliver
The house at the end of Ferry Road has just been built.
So it can't be haunted, can it. . . ?

Beware! This House is Haunted
This House is Haunted Too!
Lance Salway
Jessica doesn't believe in ghosts. So who *is* writing the
strange, spooky messages?

The Children Next Door
Jean Ure
Laura longs to make friends with the children next door.
But they're not quite what they seem. . .

The Girl in the Blue Tunic
Jean Ure
Who is the strange girl Hannah meets at school – and
why does she seem so alone?